Riders on the March

Christine
Pullein-Thompson

Riders on the March

Illustrated by Harry Lindfield

DRAGON
GRANADA PUBLISHING
London Toronto Sydney New York

Published by Granada Publishing Limited
in Dragon Books 1979

ISBN 0 583 30274 2

First published in Great Britain by
May Fair Books Ltd 1970
Copyright © Christine Pullein-Thompson 1970

Granada Publishing Limited
Frogmore, St Albans, Herts AL2 2NF
and
3 Upper James Street, London W1R 4BP
1221 Avenue of the Americas, New York, NY 10020, USA
117 York Street, Sydney, NSW 2000, Australia
100 Skyway Avenue, Toronto, Ontario, Canada M9W 3A6
110 Northpark Centre, 2193 Johannesburg, South Africa
CML Centre, Queen & Wyndham, Auckland 1, New Zealand

Printed and bound in Great Britain by
Cox & Wyman Ltd, Reading
Set in Intertype Times

Granada Publishing ®

ILLUSTRATIONS

Chapter One

Fiona was riding Buccaneer. She was tall and dark with a nose which turned up at the end, and long, artistic hands. She lived with her parents in the Manor, which once had been surrounded by fields but now stood in the midst of newer, shabbier houses, looking like a rich elderly relation among a poorer generation. Buccaneer was eight, a half-bred gelding of fifteen hands two with a large, kind eye. His mane was plaited and he wore an eggbutt snaffle.

June followed Fiona, small and fair on grey Seagull. She lived on the fourth floor of a block of flats which overlooked the riding school. She had four brothers and sisters and her jodhs were patched at the knee. Seagull belonged to the riding school. He was fourteen, wise and cunning, and an expert at gymkhana events.

James rode beside June on his bike. He was West Indian with large, sad eyes and a mouth which was usually smiling. His father worked on the railway and he lived with his two sisters in a basement. One day he meant to return to the West Indies as a jockey. In the meantime he helped whenever he could at the riding school.

Further back Alan was clattering past the gasworks on Firefly, a chestnut with two white socks and a blaze; close behind were the twins, Nancy and Naomi, whose parents kept the Anchor, a pub five minutes from the town centre.

Susan, the girl groom, brought up the rear. She wore a hairnet under her crash cap and breeches and boots. She had square shoulders and a square, patient face. She rode The Witch, a solid brown mare, and she lived in a caravan on the edge of the jumping paddock.

They were riding home from a horse show in the

7

gathering twilight. Angela Manners, the owner of the riding school, had gone ahead with her mare Moonstruck in the trailer. The street lights were on already. The shops were shut. Most people were in their houses watching television or eating supper.

"He'll do better next year," said Fiona, patting Buccaneer. "I feel it in my bones. Did you see how he jumped the gate?"

"It was my fault Seagull hit the last bending pole. I forgot to use my legs," June said.

It was always like this after shows—they all talked about their own performances without listening to each other.

James's back tyre was nearly flat. He guessed he had a puncture, but he was not going to look until he was home, back in that other world where he really belonged, in the basement where he lived; where the paper was peeling off the walls and rats raided the dustbins outside. He kept his two lives separate, no child from the riding school knew where he lived. June did much the same, only pointing to the flats vaguely, saying, "I live over there. I can see the horses from my windows." Never asking anyone to tea.

Nancy and Naomi were talking about the musical poles. Susan was tired and limp and her back ached. She had been up at six and now it was past eight in the evening and she had not sat down once all day. The Witch shied at every bit of grating in the road and there was a smell from the gasworks. Fiona was trotting now though they were nearly home. James was running with his bike, which had no lights; he ran like an athlete, his jeans hiding his thin legs. Will Mike be waiting in the caravan? wondered Susan, and imagined his bike propped up outside, the caravan smelling of cigarettes.

They were in sight of the riding school now. Fiona was turning down the short, unmade road which led to the yard gate. Then she stopped.

8

"Oh no," she shouted. "Hurry, look at this! What does it mean? It can't mean the riding school. We would have heard before. Surely someone would have told us . . ." She saw her whole life changed. The Christmas holidays barren of amusement, like a desert before her. No home for Buccaneer, no Angela Manners . . .

James could hardly read. He stared at the notice saying, "What does it mean?"

With a sinking heart June read:

5th EAST HANLEY DEVELOPMENT SCHEME
5 to 6 Storey Flats. Shops
OLD PEOPLE'S BUNGALOWS
ADVENTURE PLAYGROUND

It was a very large notice. Suddenly she started to feel sick.

Alan was tall with dark hair. He felt fury mounting in him like a rising river.

"Why didn't Angela tell us this was going to happen?" he shouted. "We might have done something. My father could have written letters to the paper. He writes marvellous letters."

"Perhaps it's all a mistake. Perhaps they put the notice in the wrong place. People do make mistakes," June said.

"We'll soon find out," shouted Fiona starting to ride down the drive.

"Perhaps she's getting a lot of money," said James, who loved Angela Manners more than anyone else in the world, his mother included. "Everybody likes money. You can't blame Angela."

"It isn't her land," Fiona shouted over her shoulder. "It belongs to her aunt, who promised never to sell. She's a dear old lady who hates progress. I can't think what can have happened." She could feel tears pricking at the backs of her eyes. "She promised," she repeated.

"It's the Council of course. They can do anything they like nowadays," Alan said, kicking Firefly until he cantered on the drive.

"You don't really believe that," replied James, who went to chapel each Sunday in suit and spotless white shirt.

"Don't canter," shouted Susan from behind. "We are nearly home and you'll ruin Firefly's legs."

James wished he could read. He still did not know exactly what had happened and now they were in the yard; he propped up his bike while the others dismounted. They all started talking at once and then Angela appeared. She spoke to Susan before she said, "You've all seen the notice I expect. I didn't want it to happen, nor did my aunt." She sounded harassed. "It's just one of those things. One can't fight the authorities, not unless you're rich, and I'm not rich. I've been lucky to have these stables all these years. We all have. You can't fight progress."

"But it isn't progress," cried Alan, taking off Firefly's saddle. "Destroying things isn't progress. Why couldn't they build their flats somewhere else, and their beastly playground for snotty-nosed kids. They could have put them where the new school's going up, over there," he cried, pointing beyond the stables into the gathering darkness. "Why do they have to ruin our lives?"

"They are like Hitler," Fiona said. "They are dictators."

"Dad's on the Council," said Nancy quietly standing with her crash cap in her hand. "And he's *not* like Hitler."

"Why didn't he do anything then?" cried Alan.

"Do you mind if I go now? My bike hasn't got a light," asked James. He was remembering his mother saying, "The Council never does anything for people like us." And now they were doing something and destroying something else. He did not know where he would go when there was no riding school any more. If it moved into the country he would never afford the bus fare, or he

10

would wear his bike tyres out riding there and he wouldn't
have money for new tyres. He felt as though he was in a
tunnel with no way out.

He pushed his bike out of the yard, past the notice
he could not read. He knew what his mother would say
already. She would say, "Now at last James we'll have
somewhere nice to live, somewhere real nice. Somewhere
you'll be proud to ask friends in. Isn't that better than a
lot of dirty fields?" And he would have to live where
the fields had once been grazed by the ponies, by Seagull,
Jetsam, Flotsam and all the others, and be grateful. I
won't say anything, he decided, for he was nearly home
now. There were boys standing at street corners and a
shop still open and a smell of diesel engines hanging over
everything. Perhaps Alan and Fiona will do something,
he thought, carrying his bike down the basement steps.
They have nice houses and Alan's father owns a factory.
They will know what to do.

"You're late," said his mother, opening the door.
"Where you been all this time? You haven't been getting
into mischief, have you?"

"I was at the horse show," he answered, and it seemed
years ago already, like a dream. "Fiona won two firsts
and a third and June was second in the musical poles . . .
Angela says that next year I can have Seagull for some
of the twelve and under classes. She says I've earned
some rides," and then he remembered the notice. "If the
riding school's still there then," he added.

"Which it won't be, Jamie darling," his mother said.
"There's going to be a playground we can all use. Isn't
that lovely, real lovely? Your sisters will be able to go
there afternoons and maybe by and by there may be a
flat for us, a real nice flat, think of that, Jamie boy," she
said. "With a proper front door, and all new with a
bathroom."

The others were still talking in the yard, while Susan led the ponies down to the dew-drenched fields. She could see the new comprehensive school rising in the distance like a giant in the dusk.

"I may be married by next year," she decided. "Or I can get another job. I shall be all right."

"My aunt did argue about the land," Angela said. She was wearing a head scarf over her shorty curly hair, an old sweater and jeans. "She could have sold it for much more for private building. She doesn't get the money anyway. It goes straight into a family trust. And they want to pull down her house."

"There should have been a public inquiry. It's ridiculous," said Alan. "I shall speak to my father. He's no fool, thank goodness! He will do something."

"Where shall I keep Buccaneer? It would be easier if I wasn't at boarding school, but I have to have someone to look after him in term," Fiona said.

"Can't you move the riding school?" asked Naomi, who like Nancy, had ginger hair, freckles and a round face and hazel eyes. "Can't you buy a farm?"

There was a short pause before Angela said, "I haven't got thirty thousand pounds. Farms are very expensive."

"Why didn't they think of a playground before they built those ghastly flats over there?" Fiona asked. "Ten years ago this was a nice little town. Now look at it!"

"I think I'll go now," June said.

"You had all better go," replied Angela. "Or your parents will be ringing up."

"We'll all meet here tomorrow," Alan said. "We will hold a Council of War. Does anyone know any M.P.s?"

"Daddy might," replied Fiona.

Buccaneer was stabled. She spoke to him before she walked away down the drive without saying goodbye to anyone, her eyes suddenly full of tears.

The street outside was full of youths in leather jackets riding motor bikes. One gave a wolf whistle as she passed;

another revved his bike and laughed. There was a moon now in the sky. The Manor House seemed to welcome her as she went inside. "I'm home," she shouted, wiping her feet on the doormat. "And have you heard the news?"

Her parents were at dinner, with table napkins, cut glass and silver cutlery.

"Come in. I'll just get your dinner out of the oven," called her mother.

"Have you heard the news?" Fiona repeated entering the dining room. "Have you heard about the riding school?"

Her father still wore his town suit. He was eating a globe artichoke with his fingers, dipping the leaves in butter and sucking them.

Fiona sat down. She was trying not to cry.

"Yes, we've known for some time," her mother said, putting a bowl of soup in front of her. "I can't think what we'll do with Buccaneer."

"We've been hoping you'd get over being so horsy," her father explained. "We thought you were getting interested in Paul, that you might not mind . . ."

"But what has Paul got to do with it? He's just a boy I know. He's not like Buccaneer," Fiona replied, and she thought, they don't understand, they never have understood. "I'm in the middle of schooling Buccaneer. He's going to the Horse Trials. I may be selected for the Pony Club team next year. He may be good enough for Badminton." She realised how little her parents knew about riding, and how much she had relied on Angela over the years. It was Angela who had chosen Buccaneer, who had found the tack to fit him, and taught her how to ride him. Her father had simply written a cheque for three hundred and fifty pounds.

"What do you think I would do all day if I hadn't Buccaneer?" she asked, sipping soup without tasting it.

Less than a hundred yards away, June was home. She had run breathlessly up four flights of stairs. And before she reached the flat she could hear the din inside. Her mother opened the door. "About time too," she cried, her hands dripping soapsuds. "I could have done with you earlier, June. What a day I've had! Jim's near cut his finger off, and your baby sister pulled all the ornaments off the mantelpiece. And here you come waltzing in at half-past eight playing the young lady."

She was wearing a pinny and fluffy bedroom slippers.

"I'm sorry, Mum. Shall I help you now? The show went on rather long; but it doesn't matter, because there isn't going to be a riding school soon. You'll have me at home to help all the time," she cried running past her mother into the bedroom which they all shared and flinging herself on the bed.

"Don't carry on so. It's not as though there isn't going to be something in its stead. There's going to be a subway, that's the latest, a subway from by these flats into the playground. There won't be any more kiddies getting killed playing on the road outside. I shan't be worried all day long. I shall be able to watch you playing from the windows; isn't that something?"

"And I shall never ride again," replied June, her voice muffled by bed clothes. "It would be different if I was like Fiona with rich parents. She will be able to go on riding holidays; but I shall never, never ride again, not properly for an hour on end. And I love grooming too. I love all of it, even the smell of horses."

She imagined the playground with logs to climb and concrete ships and tunnels. But I'm too old for adventure playgrounds, she thought, sitting up and wiping her eyes. I like the wind rushing by me as I gallop; a neck in front with pricked ears at the end.

"I've kept you some tea," her mother said. "It isn't much, but it will keep the wolf from the door."

14

"Seagull hit the last bending pole; otherwise I would have won," said June, pulling a fourth rosette from her pocket.

*   *   •   *   *

Alan was discussing the situation of the riding school with his parents. They lived in a new house with three bathrooms, four bedrooms and open plan living downstairs. His father was like him, tall, dark-haired and quick tempered. His mother was small and meek. She always agreed with everything his father said.

"The old aunt should have got a public inquiry launched right from the start," his father said. "It's a little late now, but if you can whip up enough public sympathy it might still be achieved. I suggest you start by writing a letter to the local paper. You can use my typewriter."

"I'm not much good at writing letters," replied Alan.

"Well, have a shot, and I will look it over afterwards and make any necessary alterations. You can write along the lines of a piece of Old England giving great pleasure to a great many youngsters, about the inspiration and responsibility riding gives to the young, something along those lines. And maybe one of your friends, Fiona perhaps, can write about the old lady. How she is being uprooted from her home in the twilight of her life . . . okay? Get cracking then."

Alan went into his father's study and shut the door. Thank goodness for James, he thought. At least I can put, *giving great pleasure to children of all nationalities, white and coloured alike*. He started to type and all the time he was seeing bulldozers digging up the stables and great piles of new bricks and pipes stacked in the fields. And Firefly the fastest horse in the stables going to a sale. And a playground full of toddlers and prams; and worst of all, himself at home all day with nothing to do but watch telly, go to the cinema or be a nuisance to everyone.

※   ※   •   ※   ※

The Anchor was open when the twins reached home. They entered by the back and found their mother preparing sandwiches for customers in the little kitchen behind the bar.

"Why didn't Dad do something about the riding school?" they demanded standing, still in their crash caps.

"Ssh," their mother replied. "There's supper on the table in the sitting room. I was getting worried. I rang Mrs. Manners . . ."

There was cold ham and chicken, and lettuce and baked beans on the table in the middle of the sitting room, which looked out on a small, tired piece of garden, which no one had time to tend.

"Dad should have done something for the riding school," said Nancy, sitting down. "He knows how much it means to us."

"I shall tell him Fiona says he's a Hitler, that all the Council are. He won't like that. He will have to do something then," Naomi announced.

There were antimacassars on the chairs. They could hear a man laughing in the Public Bar.

"I shall go mad without the riding school," cried Nancy, swallowing lettuce. "There won't be any point in living any more."

"There must be something we can do," replied Naomi.

Chapter Two

Fiona wakened to the sound of church bells. She could see the church from her window. It was old and grey and like the manor, stood surrounded by new houses. People were already converging on it for early Communion. Fiona jumped out of bed and almost at once she remembered the notice. I've done nothing, she thought. And there can't be much time left. She pulled on jeans and an old sweater. The sun was already up. It shone on the cups hanging on the kitchen dresser. Her parents were still in bed. Later they would go to church. Fiona made herself some toast and all the time she was thinking, we must do something quickly, we mustn't procrastinate. Her bike was in the shed by the back door. The streets were almost empty. There must be something we can do, she thought, pedalling towards the riding school, things cannot change so quickly. The church bells had stopped ringing. It was a lovely warm September morning and her heart was as heavy as lead. She tried not to look at the notice, but she saw it just the same . . . 5 *and* 6 *Storey Flats,* she read, and it was like the end of everything.

Susan and Angela were mucking out when she reached the yard. "I'll do Buccaneer's box," she said, dismounting from her bike. "I meant to get here at seven, but I didn't wake up." Suddenly every minute left at the riding school was precious. Before it had seemed to be something which would always be there, like the manor and her parents, and toast for breakfast; now nothing seemed safe from change.

17

Buccaneer whinnied when he saw her.

"I should turn him out for a bit," said Angela. "It's such a lovely morning."

There was still dew on the grass. He rolled over and over while she held the head collar and watched, thinking, where will he be next September?

Susan was singing and pushing the wheelbarrow when she returned to the yard. She was wearing a headscarf with flowers on it.

"Cheer up, Finey," she said. "Nothing goes on for ever."

And Fiona, who hated being called Finey, said, "Oh, doesn't it?" and then, "It's all right for you, you've only been here a few months. I've grown up with Angela Manners and the riding school. My best friends are here, and where shall I keep Buccaneer?" Her voice was breaking. She rushed into Buccaneer's box and shut the door.

"It may be good for you in the long run," called Susan.

Alan was coming into the yard now waving a letter. He was dressed for church in grey trousers and his best hacking jacket. "I've written a letter," he called, "it's a bit long, but the editor can cut it if he likes."

"It won't do any good," replied Angela. "They've served a C.P.O. on my aunt."

"I don't care," replied Alan, standing in the yard, his heart pounding against his ribs. "I'm not giving up, not till the flats start rising and the stables are gone."

He read the letter to Fiona in Buccaneer's loose box.

"Sir," he began, "Many people are profoundly shocked to learn of the proposal to develop the land so long used by Miss Angela Manners for her riding school. I wish to object on several counts:—

1. Loss of amenity to the whole riding community which is made up of all classes and all nationalities;
2. Loss of open space in an area which has little enough;
3. Change of character of the whole area;

18

4. Lack of consultation on the scheme with the nearby residents.

       Yours truly, etc. etc.," he finished.

"It's a marvellous letter," Fiona said, "though I don't understand all of it. I mean nobody used it as an open space except us."

"That doesn't matter. It was still an area of beauty and fresh air," replied Alan. I'm going to post it now. Then I am going to church. I want us all to meet here for a proper discussion after lunch. Tell anyone who turns up. Three o'clock in the saddle room."

He stopped to pat Firefly. He had hardly slept all night, for the letter had gone on writing itself in his head long after it was written. He turned and looked at the fields before he left, imagining the first piece of turf cut, the beginning of the end.

"Don't forget, three o'clock," he called over his shoulder. "I haven't had breakfast yet . . ." He was running now, past the hated notice, wondering if his letter would ever be published.

"What's a C.P.O.?" asked Fiona, shaking Buccaneer's straw with a pitchfork.

"Compulsory purchase order. It means the Council can buy at their own price, or almost, whatever my aunt says. Like in a police state," replied Angela. "I tell you, it's hopeless, Fiona," she continued. "I've seen a solicitor, and anyway my aunt's too old to fight. She says she's going to an old peoples' home. She doesn't want to start again somewhere else in a new house of her own."

"We can raise a petition," Fiona answered. "There must be people who will sign it."

"Some, but not enough. I shall go right away from here. I don't want to see the houses going up. I can sell the boxes; they're portable . . ." Angela said. There were dark circles under her eyes and the lines on her face had deepened. Suddenly she seemed older and sadder. "I shan't teach any more," she added.

19

Fiona could not think of anything to say. She wished that her mother was there, for her mother always had the right word for every occasion. "We're not going to let it happen," she said. "We'll stop it somehow."

And Angela simply gave a wan smile which seemed to enlarge the hollows in her wan cheeks. "Alan has strong friends and Naomi and Nancy's father is a councillor. We're going to fight to the bitter end." Fiona was trying not to cry; what she said sounded feeble even to herself. But now James was coming into the yard wheeling his battered bicycle, looking sad and lanky with the laughter knocked out of his face.

"Anything happen?" he called hopefully. "Has Alan done something? What did your mother and father say, Fiona?"

"We're going to meet here at three o'clock," said Fiona. "Alan's written a letter to the paper."

"I knew he would do something," James replied with admiration in his voice. "Is there anything I can do for you, Angela?"

"Well, there's yesterday's tack," replied Angela. "If you can bear it."

He wanted to cheer up Angela. "Things will come right," he said. "I prayed for you this morning at early service. I went there specially." He had gone with the rest of the family. After the service he had run home ahead, and changed into old clothes and come straight to the stables before anyone could stop him, only stopping to spit at the notice by the gate.

He loved the smell of saddle soap. He stood cleaning the tack, glad he had escaped from the basement, which was dim inside even on the sunniest morning.

Susan was going out. "Well, I'll leave you to it," she said, poking her head in the tack room door. "Don't get into any mischief and remember the world won't end because the stables go." And suddenly James hated her.

She's ignorant, he thought. She does not care for Angela. Can't she see it's half killing her?

"I've brought my dinner," he said to no one in particular. "I shall be here all day; so don't worry, Fiona, I won't miss the meeting."

He had helped himself to half a loaf of bread and a great wedge of cheese. He had split the bread in two and carried it unwrapped in the pocket of his blazer.

Fiona was going now. "I'm going to ring up Naomi and Nancy," she said. "I don't know how to get hold of June. She lives in the new flats, doesn't she?"

James nodded. He had cleaned a bridle already. "What will happen to Angela's house?" he asked and they both turned to look at it.

"They may leave it. Who knows?" replied Fiona.

It had once been the lodge. It was Victorian like the large house where Angela's aunt still lived with a companion. Fiona looked at the sky. "I'll leave Buccaneer till I come back," she said, mounting her bicycle, pedalling away leaving James alone with the horses and the sunshine in the place he loved, more than anywhere else on earth. He continued cleaning the tack, trying not to think beyond the moment, listening to Firefly eating hay in the box next door, pretending to himself that nothing had happened; but it was no use, for he kept hearing Angela's exhausted voice, seeing the notice he could not read, and it was like nightmare without end.

           ◦   ◦   •   ◦   ◦

"It's for one of you, either of you. It doesn't matter. It sounds like Fiona," said Mrs. Frome. It was opening time and there was a deafening noise in the saloon bar.

"I'll answer," said Nancy. She picked up the receiver in the sitting room. "What is it?" she asked.

"Fiona speaking. Alan wants us to meet this afternoon

21

at three o'clock in the tack room. Can you both come?" she asked.

"Who is it? Is it Fiona? What's happened?" interrupted Naomi.

"Yes, of course. We'll come. We'll set out directly after dinner," shouted Nancy. "Has anything happened?"

"Nothing marvellous," answered Fiona. "See you then."

"What did she want?" asked Mrs. Frome, who was wearing high heels, black skirt, mauve sweater and pearls.

"There's going to be a meeting in the tack room. Can we have an early dinner?"

"Not till closing time," replied Mrs. Frome, returning to the saloon bar.

"We'll have to get something ourselves. We can catch the two o'clock bus," Naomi said. "What shall we say about Daddy? I feel so ashamed of him, don't you?"

"Terribly," agreed Nancy. "I'm going to get ready now."

§   §   •   §'   §

"Don't come in. It's in a terrible mess," said June with wide, horrified eyes. "How did you know I lived here?"

"I made inquiries. There's a meeting this afternoon in the tack room at three o'clock. Can you come?" Fiona asked.

"Yes, if Mum will let me. Yes, anyway, somehow. I wish you hadn't come," June said. Her baby sister was standing behind her without any shoes. "I don't like people coming here."

"I can't think why. Lots of people live in flats. You can't help living in a flat. It's just one of those things. What difference does it make?" asked Fiona. "Everybody has to live somewhere. See you at three then." She was glad to run down the winding concrete stairs. The air felt fresher when she was outside again. Glad I don't live here, she thought.

"I've got to go out this afternoon," June told her mother. I don't care what you say, or Dad. I've got to go."

"But it's Sunday," replied her mother. "You always take the kiddies out on a Sunday afternoon."

"Not this Sunday. I can't. Soon they'll have me every Sunday, for years and years, and Saturdays too, so you can't spoil this one Sunday, can you?"

"No, it's all right," replied her mother, suddenly different. "If it's important you go, my duck. I can manage."

"I must know what's happening," said June going to the window, seeing the stables, small like toy stables, far below with the fields like patchwork beyond. Buccaneer was standing under a clump of trees, near the shallow pit which they used as a cross country drop fence. He looked like a toy too; and beyond it all, the new comprehensive school was growing. "I wish nothing ever changed, Mum," she said.

"You had better have your dinner now and get going," her mother replied. "Heaven knows when your Dad will be in."

    :   :   .   :   :

Alan was helping himself to his father's foolscap paper. He wrote at the top of each page, PETITION IN CONNECTION WITH SAVING THE RIGHTWAY STABLES FROM COMPULSORY PURCHASE ORDER. He had wanted to ask his father what to write, but his parents had gone out to lunch with friends, leaving him a cold lunch in the larder.

He had taken an opened packet of foolscap paper and there were twenty-five pages inside. He reckoned that would be enough to begin with. We can go from door to door, he thought. There must be millions of people

23

who feel like we do. I should have asked the rector, he thought, fetching his lunch from the larder. The sun was shining through the large windows in the living room. Alan read yesterday's *Horse and Hound* as he ate . . . Then he tipped his plates into the sink and set off for the stables, the foolscap paper under his arm.

Chapter Three

They were all in the tack room. James had cleaned all the tack. It hung gleaming on the walls. The yard outside was swept clean; there was not a wisp of straw to be seen anywhere. The horses were dozing in their boxes. Flies buzzed outside. The curtains were drawn in the lodge.

"She's ill," James said. "She's killing herself with worry."

"Which is why we're here," replied Alan.

The horses always rested after a gymkhana. It was one of Angela's "golden rules". I could be so happy, thought Fiona, if only it could all stay the same.

Most of them were wearing jeans. Alan took the foolscap paper from under his arm.

"This is for the petition," he announced. "I hope you agree with the heading. I suggest we each start with one sheet and try to get fifty signatures."

"You mean people to write their names?" asked James.

Alan nodded. "Has anyone else done anything?"

Nancy turned red. "We've been very rude to Daddy," she said.

"Well perhaps *you* had better have several sheets; one for each bar," suggested Alan.

"We can try," replied Naomi doubtfully.

"I'll have two," said Fiona.

"I don't know anyone who will sign," said June. "I don't know any well-off people. Well, Fiona knows where I live ..."

"But you must do something," cried Alan. "You can't

25

just sit there. No one cares where you live. Did Angela care? Of course she didn't. Surely your Mum will sign. What about your brothers and sisters?"

"They can't write."

"What, none of them?"

"They're too young," replied June.

"Perhaps the baker will, or the milkman. Try everybody," Alan said. "Anybody got any other suggestions?"

James looked at his feet. He could think of nothing; he was filled with a great sadness; his eyes wandered to the tack and he thought, I cleaned it all for Angela, but she won't notice, she doesn't notice anything any more.

"Speak up," shouted Alan, sounding like his father. "I can't do everything. I've written to the paper, now I've got the petition ready..."

June was remembering something Mum had once said. It was at Christmas time. She had stood in the kitchen and shouted, "I don't know why your Uncle Stan never sends you anything. Him an M.P. and all. And they've just voted themselves more money . . . He must be doing all right."

"My uncle is an M.P.," she announced so quietly that the others hardly heard her. "He lives in London."

"An M.P!" shouted Alan. "Just the job. "We had better see him. We can all go . . ."

"I haven't seen him for years," replied June. "He must be quite old. He's really a great-uncle."

"That doesn't matter," said Alan, writing in a notebook.

"I don't even remember him."

"That doesn't matter either. Get his address. We'll go in old clothes, looking poor. I expect he's Labour," Alan replied.

"I will have to ask Mum for his address," June said, wondering how they would get to London, what Mum would say when they went, what Dad would say, how Mum would manage without her.

26

"I have a suggestion," said Fiona. "I suggest we march through the town to the Town Hall. On horses. We can begin here and go right through the centre, down the high street, through the Market Place." She could see it already in her mind—all Angela's horses, Buccaneer leading, two by two carrying banners . . .

"That's fantastic," cried Alan. "There's going to be a meeting quite soon. I'll get the date from my father."

"We'll all go," cried Naomi. "We can go past the Anchor."

"Dad will be at the meeting," Nancy said.

"Who cares?" cried Naomi. "I don't care if he's cross with us."

"Will we have to pay for the ponies?" asked James. But no one heard him. "Can anyone play a musical instrument? I wish we could hire the town band," Alan said.

"If Angela agrees to us doing it at all," replied Fiona.

"I suppose we'll have to ask," Alan said.

"We can't just take the horses and we'll need some of her pupils," Fiona answered. "I can ask George and Peter to come on their ponies.

"I can play an accordion," James said.

"We could stand and play outside the Town Hall, like the town band do on Sundays," June said.

They were all standing up now, fired with enthusiasm.

"Everyone got a sheet of paper?" Alan asked. And they all nodded. "Tomorrow you can each take another. Let's get cracking," he cried.

"What about June's great-uncle? "There's the Horse Trials next Saturday," Fiona said.

"We will go next Sunday then. You had better write to him, June. We will get there somehow," Alan replied. He felt in control now. We'll fight to the end, he thought.

Fiona crossed the yard and walked down to the fields to catch Buccaneer. The cavaletti were in a line waiting to be jumped. The dressage arena was in place. Saturday was less than a week away. It was the end of a year's schooling; she had been dreaming of it for months; now suddenly it was pushed into the background, over-shadowed by the petition and the march. We can call it the March of the Riders, she thought. Buccaneer whinnied when he saw her. She vaulted onto his back and rode back to the stables.

The sun was dipping in the west now, a big summer sun as red as an orange. The others had gone already, their sheets of paper in their hands like weapons. And supposing it doesn't work? wondered Fiona. Supposing no one wants to sign?

Angela was coming out of the lodge now. "Have they all gone already?" she asked.

Fiona nodded. "Shall I give him the usual feed?" she asked, leading Buccaneer into his box.

"I should. We'll go through the dressage tomorrow and do the cross country. We'll have the last practice on Thursday. Friday you can hack him," she said.

She was going too, riding her grey mare Moonstruck. She leaned on Buccaneer's door and looked at Fiona. "I'm sorry about all this," she said. "We must find somewhere else for Buccaneer."

"There isn't anywhere else," replied Fiona. "I've thought for hours in bed ever since I saw the notice, there isn't anywhere suitable."

"It's awful for me too," replied Angela. "It's my whole life going. I sit and sit in the evenings, and think and think and it's like someone dying. I'm numb. I can't make plans. I can't believe all this is simply going to be taken and pulled down. It seems so wanton somehow."

Don't cry, thought Fiona, or I shall cry too. "We're not going to let it happen," she answered, running her hands down Buccaneer's clean tendons to hide the tears rising in her eyes.

"You can't stop it happening," said Angela. "It's

happening all the time. People can be turned out of their houses so that a road can be widened."

"We've got plans," replied Fiona mysteriously.

But Angela had gone now and the sun had set. Fiona fed Buccaneer, found her bicycle and rode home. Her parents signed the petition and then she rang up Paul, who said, was it too late for the cinema? Fiona said that it was, but that she had a petition for him to sign; and presently he came with a scarf pushed into an open-necked shirt and corduroys.

"I've heard about the stables," he said. "I'm ready to sign your petition, but I don't really agree with it. People must have houses, and there is still plenty of sub-standard housing in this town."

He was tall with glasses. Suddenly Fiona hated him "You sign here," she said, pushing the sheet of foolscap paper under his nose.

"You haven't got many signatures so far," he said, writing Paul Johnson in a small, squiggly hand.

"They should move the people to a new town, not spoil this one," she answered. "They are going to build blocks of flats. People hate living in them. I called on one today. It was awful. The washing was hanging in the balcony and there was no garden for the children. They should build proper villages with gardens and a green . . .

"Life isn't like that. There's the question of money and land," began Paul, and to stop him lecturing her she said, "Would you like a bitter lemon, or is it tea time?"

.   .   .   .   .

James stood holding the sheet of paper. "Can you sign this?" he asked without much hope.

His father took it. He put on his glasses and read the typing at the top. "No, I can't, son," he said. "It ain't possible." And he knew his mother would not sign it either now.

"We might get offered a house there," his father said. "This isn't no place to bring up a family."

James remembered the tack room, the smell of the clean tack, everyone standing up. Anything had seemed possible then, even his parents signing. He carried the piece of paper into the bedroom and put it under his pillow.

"You won't get anyone to sign it," his mother said, when he had sat down at the table in the centre of the room. No one in this town will. We want new houses. I'm sorry, Jamie boy."

"The others will," James said. "We're going to see a Member of Parliament. We are going to London."

They did not believe him. "We are going to march through the town on horses and I'm going to play the accordion," he said and suddenly the chair he sat on was a saddle between his legs, the spars like stirrups.

They laughed, and continued laughing, but he hardly heard them. He imagined instead the hoofs of ponies clattering down the high street . . . the mayor coming out of the Town Hall with his chain of office on to receive the petition. "We are going to fight," he said, but they were still laughing.

"That would really be something," his mother cried. "You and your old accordion outside the Town Hall!"

.   .   .   .   .

The Anchor was not open yet. Nancy and Naomi took their copies of the petition straight into the bars.

"We'll stick them up with drawing pins," Naomi said.

Nancy made two small notices saying, SAVE THE RIDING SCHOOL. SIGN PLEASE, and pinned them to the wall too, and hung pencils nearby. The bars smelt of beer and cigarettes. Naomi held her nose, exclaiming, "Oh, for the smell of horses?"

Nancy said, "Supposing Daddy pulls them down and throws them in the fire?"

"We can get more copies from Alan tomorrow. We've got a lesson at half-past ten."

They crept out of the bars on tiptoes for their parents were resting upstairs. They found some swiss roll in the larder and ate it.

"I bags Seagull for the march," Naomi said.

"If Angela lets us march at all," replied Nancy. "Fancy June having an M.P. uncle. Her father is only a municipal dustman you know."

"I was surprised too," Naomi said. "Daddy will never believe us if we tell him. Ssh. He's coming down now."

"We had better hide."

They rushed into the larder and shut the door. They heard him go into the saloon bar. They crept to the door and listened. There was the sound of glasses clinking together. Then he said, "For Pete's sake what's this?" and they shrank back from the door and listened. "He's tearing them down," Naomi whispered.

Later he swung the door open. He was a big man with large hands. "What's this?" he demanded. "Do you want to drive all my customers away? I'm a councillor. I have responsibilities. I was there when the whole thing was discussed. Do you want me to lose my licence?"

They had come out of the larder and were standing in the kitchen. He had all three petitions in his hand. He tore them into shreds and threw them on the sitting room fire. "You're getting too keen on riding, that's what it is," he said. "You don't think of anything else."

"There isn't anything else to think of," replied Naomi.

"There isn't anything else to do," said Nancy.

"June's got an uncle who is an M.P. We are going to see him. But you won't do anything to help, even though you *are* a councillor," Naomi said.

"And June's father is a municipal dustman."

"How does she manage to ride then?" he asked.

31

"She works in exchange for rides," Naomi said.

"I can't help. This pub belongs to the brewery. They want more houses, more houses mean more business," their father said and suddenly Naomi thought, he's trapped too, we are all trapped by something.

   ⁂ • ⁂ ⁂ ⁂

"I'll sign it, of course, duck," June's mother said. "But your Dad won't, and I don't know anyone else who will. We all want a subway, duck. There, will that do?" she asked, handing June back the sheet of paper. "I'm afraid it's a lost cause, duck. Never mind, we'll go to the sea come the summer and you can ride on the sands."

"The sands!" cried June. "The sands after going for mock hunts and to shows, after galloping round a ring with a rosette in your mouth and everyone clapping. Oh Mum!"

She put her anorak on to go out again, but her mother said, "Oh, no more of that. You've been out all afternoon, now you stop in a bit. I need a hand—there's all the ironing and your Dad's coming in for his tea any minute."

"I wanted to get some more signatures," June said.

"You won't get any, duck. You've done enough for Angela Manners for one day."

"It's not for her. It's for all of us. For the ponies too. They will have to be sold if the stables are knocked down. And when we look out of the windows we won't see fields any more. Don't you even care about that, Mum?" June cried.

"Listen, there's your Dad coming back with the kids," her mother said. "Put the kettle on."

June was depressed now. It is all right for Alan and Fiona, she thought, they are used to getting their own way. People do what they say. But who will sign the petition for me? The evening sun shone on the windows. It showed up the dirt on the window panes. She could see Angela crossing the stable yard, a bucket in her hand. We will just see other windows, other flats, more washing, she thought. I shall have to stand here, watching the buildings grow, and remembering . . .

   ⦂   •   ⦂   ⦂   ⦂

Alan had nine signatures already. He was filled with jubilation. We'll win yet, he thought. The houses he called on were mostly new. They had fancy door bells which went ding dong and garaging for two cars. Their gardens were full of autumn flowers wilting beneath the setting sun. He stood waiting outside the door of his fourth house. Its owners knew him and they welcomed him as a friend.

"Of course we'll sign," they exclaimed when they heard the reason for his visit. "We love seeing the horses. More flats would change the character of the area completely."

The whole family signed, including the au pair girl. Seven more signatures, he thought, hurrying down the crazy paving path. But we need hundreds more. And on Saturday I shall be at the Horse Trials with Angela and Fiona. His parents were home waiting dinner for him. "We are going to see an M.P. next Sunday," he told them. Perhaps he will write to the *Times*, or ask a question in the House of Commons. I'm getting on fine with the petition. I think we'll win."

"Give me a copy and I'll take it to the golf club," his father said, eating cold meat. "They will sign for fear of being the next victim."

"We are going to organise a march. We'll have to ask the police, I suppose?"

He was imagining himself now walking up the steps of the Town Hall, bowing before the mayor, handing him sheets and sheets of foolscap paper, while the horses and riders stood by the steps below waiting for him like an army.

33

Chapter Four

June was running towards the riding school. She was wearing the jodhpurs her mother had bought from Fiona's mother's jumble sale. They had once belonged to Naomi. In her pocket she carried ten shillings in silver for her lesson.

"I saved it from the children's allowances," her mother had said. "It's really meant for clothes or food, but I reckoned riding meant more to you than either."

"Yes, you were right," June had agreed. "I only want riding clothes, and I don't care about food. I would rather go barefoot than give up riding."

And her mother sighed, muttering, "I wish you had never started it."

Alan will be furious, thought June, seeing the riding school in the distance. But I can't help it. I did try. Rosie, her youngest sister, had found the petition and scribbled on it; then the baby had pulled it to pieces. But now a car was stopping. A man leaned out of the window, and June thought, I'm not taking a lift, not from a strange man. He wore glasses and had curly hair. "Is this the way to the riding school?" he asked.

June looked him up and down. He's from the builders, she thought. He's going to decide where the houses will go.

"No, it isn't," she replied. "You must go back through the town."

"Oh dear, I've been through it twice already," he replied, turning his car with a crunch of tyres. He looked hot and angry. "They told me to come this way," he shouted. "The lunatics . . ."

Fiona was already there when June reached the yard.

34

She was leading Seagull up and down. His dappled grey coat was wet with sweat. "He's got colic," she said. "He had it when Angela went down to the field this morning. We are all praying that he hasn't twisted a gut. If he has, he will have to be shot."

"Oh no!" shouted June covering her face with her hands. "Can't I lead him? I like him best of all the ponies."

"You are not strong enough. He keeps trying to roll," Fiona answered. "Angela has gone to telephone the vet." His nostrils were dilated, his eyes wild and delirious.

"He left half an hour ago," Angela said returning. "It's one thing after another, isn't it? I don't know why he's being so long."

June remembered the man in the car and felt sick suddenly. "Does he wear spectacles?" she asked. "Because there was a man looking for the stables, but I thought he was a builder so I told him to go back through the town."

"I don't know what he looks like. The usual one is on holiday," Angela replied. Her face was covered with a rash.

"I didn't know. I was only trying to help," June said.

"But it doesn't. They'll find their way in the end," replied Angela. "Before you can turn round they'll have their huts here and piles of bricks and lorries . . . Let me lead Seagull now. He looks a bit better, perhaps the drench is beginning to work."

"What's happened to her face?" June whispered to Fiona. But Fiona only shouted, "Here's the vet." And the man in spectacles drove into the yard and leapt out of his car with an enormous flourish, crying, "There's some sort of conspiracy going on. No one wanted to tell me the way here."

"It's a long story," Angela replied. "But here's the pony. I think he's a little better." And she turned to wink at June.

35

Susan was grooming the ponies for the ten o'clock ride and June helped her. The day was hot already. The ponies' legs were speckled with fly eggs.

"Angela's cracking up," Susan said. "Have you seen her face?"

June nodded. "How did it happen?" she asked.

"She's upset. She says it's stress, and all she needs is a bit more sleep, but I think it is more than that," replied Susan sounding pleased. "I think she is going mad with worry."

Flotsam had neat round feet. He was Dartmoor with a small white star on his forehead. June buried her face in his side. He had a wonderful smell, the most wonderful smell in the world, except for Seagull, who smelt like a wet hen when he was wet. June thought of other smells, of nappies boiling in a bucket, of cabbage kept too long, or the smell of old potato peelings, or from the exhaust of cars. I wish I could stay here for ever, she thought, that life would stop now with my face as it is. buried in his coat.

"She'll have to see the doctor," continued Susan in a loud, happy voice. "She can't go on as she is."

"You sound so happy," replied June, lifting her face from Flotsam's coat. "Aren't you sorry for her at all?"

She started to pick out Flotsam's hoofs, while Susan said, "I don't know what you mean. What a thing to say."

"I mean, it's terrible for her, isn't it? She might take her own life. Have you thought of that?" It was like someone else talking. "It's enough to kill her. It's everything she cares for going," June finished, straightening her back and looking round the yard.

The vet was leaving. Alan had come, so had James, Naomi and Nancy. They all stood talking to Fiona and June joined them.

"I got seventeen signatures. What about the rest of you?" Alan asked.

He felt wonderful this morning. "I can smell victory,"

he added. "I got lots of support yesterday evening. Everyone wanted to sign."

"I can only see the cut turf, the wooden pegs and nowhere for Buccaneer," Fiona replied. "I've only got two signatures. I'm no good at signatures. Our help wouldn't sign this morning. She said I was selfish, that kiddies were more important than my horse."

Alan's spirits fell like a barometer turning from fine to rain. "And what about you, James?" he asked.

James hung his head. "Neither mother nor father would sign," he said.

"And you didn't try anyone else?" cried Alan impatiently. "What about you two?" he shouted, glaring at Naomi and Nancy.

"We put them in the bars," Nancy replied.

"In all three?" Alan asked.

They nodded.

"And how many signatures were there this morning? Or didn't you look?"

"Daddy tore them down. He put them on the fire. It wasn't our fault," Naomi replied.

"Mum signed mine, but then Rosie got it," June said. "I'm sorry. You will have to give me another one. I'll get Mum to sign again. Then I'll go from door to door."

Alan sighed. "It's hopeless, isn't it?" he asked. "Angela's right."

"Can other people sign, or do they have to live here," Fiona asked. "I mean, couldn't we take them to the Horse Trials? All the horsy people would sign."

"That's an idea," Alan said. "Of course we can. Nobody need put their addresses."

Susan was tacking up the ponies for the ten o'clock ride. More pupils were arriving. The vet had given Seagull an injection of morphia and an enema. He was standing in one of the boxes looking small and sleepy. June stood looking at him over the door. She thought, I shall never forget this moment as long as I live. I shall always remember him as the pony who taught me to ride, and one day I shall be rich and I shall buy my children a pony just like him. He'll be Seagull the second . . .

Fiona was tacking up Buccaneer, running through the dressage test in her mind. James knew that Angela was ill. He could see it in her eyes. She seemed suddenly a completely different person. Her small, clear-cut face had disappeared beneath the rash and he could hardly see her eyes because of the swelling round them. And I'm not doing anything to help, he thought.

June pulled up Flotsam's girth and mounted. She led the way into the schooling paddock. wishing she was on Seagull. Naomi struggled onto Trooper. Nancy rode Jetsam who was a bright bay with black points. There were three other pupils, but they only arrived at the last moment, climbing out of elegant cars, taking their ponies from Susan who adjusted their stirrups and followed them into the paddock. Really it was like any other Monday morning, except that tension hung over everything, making June sit straighter than usual, James jump at every remark expecting a hidden barb. It made Fiona slap Buccaneer when he put his head too high to bridle and Alan shout at Firefly when he would not stand to be mounted. James followed the riders into the paddock. He stood behind Angela listening. He thought, I can't visit June's uncle because I have no money for the fare. If only Angela was helping in the fight everything would be different. Angela can move mountains, but Alan only shouts and loses his temper.

Fiona rode Buccaneer round the field on a loose rein. Susan was putting up the cross country fences. She rode into the dressage arena and practised halting in the centre. Alan cantered Firefly round and round in an endless circle, waiting for Angela to instruct him. I'll ride in the front of the march, he decided. But James must lead. We must find a lot more riders; we'll need twenty at least and tonight we must start making banners. Surely Fiona

38

can sew. We'll carry the Union Jack as well, he thought, to show that we believe in England, England as it was at least. He felt on edge and Firefly could feel it. I shall never manage the dressage test, he thought, I can't concentrate today.

Susan took over the class while Angela instructed Alan and Fiona. Her face was redder than ever now and her hands looked puffy. Alan could not make Firefly stand still while he took off his hat and bowed at the beginning of the dressage test; and Buccaneer refused at the drop fence and all the time it was growing hotter. Susan took the ten o'clock class back to the stables and the eleven o'clock class appeared, including six pupils riding their own ponies. They had seen the notice and could talk of nothing else. "We won't have anywhere to jump," they cried, and "Who will teach us?"

"We are going to fight," June told them. "We are getting a petition signed and we're going to march through the town. We want you to join us."

"I don't know what's the matter with you both," shouted Angela. "Neither of you can remember the test and you are both hopeless across country. You were so good last week."

"I'm sorry. Shall I do the test again?" Fiona asked.

"No," cried Angela. "He's stale now. Your extended trot is appalling. He looks like a worn-out cab horse; and Firefly's over-collected." She stared round the field and her eyes were hardly visible in her swollen face. "I can't go on," she said. "I'm sorry, I can't even see properly with this awful rash. I'll have to go indoors. The sun is making it worse every minute." She stumbled away across the field with James following, saying, "Please, can I do something?"

And suddenly Fiona could not speak. There seemed to be a lump growing larger and larger in her throat. Alan sat using all the bad language he was not allowed to use at home, and he thought, we won't go on Saturday now.

So we won't get lots of extra signatures; and all this dressage and cross country practice will be in vain.

He and Fiona rode back to the stables without speaking. Susan was still taking the eleven o'clock class and a small boy with glasses had fallen off and no one could find his glasses.

"She's very ill," Fiona said, leading Buccaneer into his box. "It would be better if she screamed or wrote rude letters, but it's all bottled up."

June was leading Seagull up and down. "He's got colic again," she said. "He was rolling in his box. What do you think we had better do?"

"I'll ask Angela," Fiona replied. "I expect the morphia's worn off and the pain has come back." She felt much older suddenly.

"If Angela's going to be ill we will have to take over," Alan said. "Susan is half-witted. She only cares about Mike."

"I don't know how she can. I couldn't stand his spots," replied Fiona.

Nancy and Naomi appeared in the yard with the small boy. "He's broken his glasses. He can't see anything without them. Someone will have to telephone his parents. Where's Angela?" asked Naomi.

"Ill indoors," Fiona answered.

"You'll have to do the telephoning," Alan said. "Just go in and use it. We can't leave Seagull how he is."

"I don't know his name," Fiona said.

"I'm Peter Andrews and my telephone number is Lumsden 2000," said the boy. "Mummy's having her hair done. She was picking me up on her way home."

"There's no point in telephoning then," Fiona answered. "She may be under the drier, or already on her way." She stood staring at Seagull. He was kicking at his stomach and there were dark patches of sweat behind his ears. She walked slowly to the lodge wondering what she would say. She knocked on the green door but no one answered, so she went inside and called "Angela, Seagull's worse. Shall I telephone the vet?" There was an odd noise coming from upstairs but no one answered.

There was rush matting in the hall and a notice above the telephone with telephone numbers on it—VET, HORSEBOX, BUTCHER, GROCER, SADDLER, CORN MERCHANT. Fiona picked up the telephone and dialled the vet's number. A woman answered.

"I'm speaking for Mrs. Manners from the Rightway Riding School," Fiona said. "You sent someone round to look at a pony this morning with colic. He's worse again."

And the woman said, "Say your name again," and then, "Oh yes, it was Mr. Chivers. I will get him on the radio; he'll be there directly."

Fiona said, "Thank you very much," and put down the receiver. She could hear Angela crying upstairs. She stood feeling worried, seeing Angela's swollen face again in her mind's eye. Then Susan came charging into the hall. "Where's Angela?" she shouted. "Is she all right? She was talking about killing herself last night. You ring the doctor while I go upstairs. And keep your voice down. Tell him to come. My uncle committed suicide, so I know what I'm talking about."

Fiona picked up the telephone again. Susan was upstairs now, charging about the room overhead. Alan poked his head round the door. "Is the vet coming? Seagull's worse," he asked.

"Yes," shouted Fiona. "But be quiet, I'm ringing Angela's doctor."

"Ask for Doctor Forest," Susan called down the stairs.

Doctor Forest answered. He promised to come at once. Fiona put down the receiver and went out into the bright sunshine, which made the grass seem greener and the sky bluer.

James was dealing with three parents who wanted to book more lessons.

"You had best ring up," he said. "Mrs. Manners is not well; she was taken bad this morning."

June was leading Seagull up and down, hitting him when he tried to roll, stifling back the tears which threatened because of the awfulness of everything.

Naomi and Nancy were feeding the ponies with anxious faces, talking only in whispers. The children on their own ponies had disappeared, leaving only a trail of hoof marks on the dusty drive.

"Is she better?" Alan asked.

"I don't know. Susan is with her. The doctor's coming at once. Everything's breaking up, isn't it?" Fiona asked.

"No. We are just going through a bad patch," Alan replied. "Margaret and Jean are coming on the march. I've fixed it for Saturday week. There's an exhibition in the Town Hall and the mayor's opening it."

"I thought marches were held on Sundays," Fiona answered. "The market will be on."

"But there won't be anyone in the Town Hall on a Sunday," replied Alan.

And suddenly Fiona did not care. She kept thinking, supposing Angela goes mad? What will happen then?

"We won't tell the police, we'll just march. It will seem more spontaneous that way," Alan said, before they both saw that Seagull was down on the gravel rolling, while June pulled on his head collar and shouted helplessly. James rushed from the saddle room, colliding with Fiona, and they all started pulling and heaving and shouting, "Get up, will you. Get up." June hit him and went on hitting, seeing without caring that the rope had torn her hands and they were bleeding. Naomi and Nancy rushed across the yard to greet Doctor Forest, who had arrived. He was tall and dark, wearing a suit and carrying a case.

"She's in the lodge," they shouted. "Her face is all swollen up."

He ran like someone not used to running. And now Seagull was standing up, sweat dripping off his sides, which were going in and out like bellows, his eyes seeming to wait with terror in them for the next spasm of pain. And June was crying now. "He's in agony," she shouted. "There must be something we can do."

"He's coming," Fiona said. "I telephoned."

"Can't you telephone again?" shouted June. Please . . ."

Fiona went indoors. She could hear Doctor Forest talking to Angela in a low voice. "He's going to take her to hospital," said Susan, who was standing in the hall.

"Seagull's worse. I'm ringing the vet again," Fiona said, and suddenly she felt calm in a desolate, bemused way.

The same woman answered. "He will be there directly," she said. "I got him on the radio. He won't be long."

"The pony is in awful agony," she said. "I think he must have twisted a gut. Can you get him again?"

"I'll try," the woman replied. "But he may have switched his radio off."

Angela was coming downstairs with Doctor Forest when Fiona put down the receiver. She was wearing dark glasses and a scarf over her hair.

She did not look at Fiona. "She said, "I'm so sorry. Try to keep everything going. Help Susan. But don't bother with pupils. Just keep the ponies fed."

"She's going to rest for a few days. You can manage, can't you?" asked Doctor Forest in a bright, professional voice. "Just keep things ticking over."

"Of course we can. Don't you worry," said Susan, who was following with a suitcase in her hand. "You have a good rest, Angela."

The vet had come again. He said, "So there you are, Mrs. Manners. I think the little chap will be all right."

"Mrs. Manners isn't well," said Alan. "You can give me any necessary instructions."

James followed the doctor's car to the end of the drive. He waved but Angela never turned her head. It's almost

43

as though we never knew each other he thought, walking sadly back along the drive.

The day seemed to have lasted for ever though it was only lunch time. Fiona wanted to sit down with her head in her hands. She wanted to think things over. Alan put Seagull back in his loose box. The vet went into the lodge with Susan to wash his hands.

"We won't be going to the Horse Trials, will we?" Fiona asked. "It's awful, but I don't really mind. Somehow it doesn't really matter compared to everything else."

Chapter Five

They ate lunch together in the saddle room and discussed the march. Alan wanted long banners carried by two riders.

"I will provide the cloth, if someone will sew them onto the poles," he said.

"Mum will. She's a wonderful sewer," June replied.

"I will paint on the cloth first," Alan said. "Shall I put SAVE THE RIDING SCHOOL?"

"Or NO MORE HOUSES," suggested Fiona.

"Mum wouldn't sew anything with that on," replied June quickly. "You see her youngest sister, Auntie Christine, had only one room and a bathroom and she's got two children and a husband."

"We could do with a better place too," James said, suddenly glad to speak about it. "But not here," he added, looking across the yard to the fields on each side of the drive where Flotsam and Jetsam stood nose to tail under the trees. "I couldn't live here in a new house."

"We had better clean the tack," said Fiona, pushing her sandwich paper into the pocket of her jodhs. "It's eerie without Angela, isn't it?"

"It spoils everything," replied James. "But we can make the place lovely for her return." He saw her coming back, a suitcase in her hand. Staring round the yard which was swept clean and the ponies perfectly groomed, all the tack cleaned so that it gleamed and shone. I will even clean the windows, he thought, and wash her car. Everything will be perfect, so that she will feel better at once and filled with a new hope, ready to fight with the rest of us for the stables.

"We must make some money for her while she's in hospital," said Naomi picking up the diary. "I see the blacksmith is coming and there's three classes . . . We'll have to get here very early; Nancy and I will catch the first bus and catch The Witch and Jasmine and Tom-tit on the way. Susan will never have time to fetch them, and they are down for all three classes."

"I'll help her with the mucking out," Fiona said. "But are you sure you'll be able to manage them?"

"Of course we can. We'll take the head collars home with us. There won't be a lot of traffic about early in the morning and if soppy old Susan can ride one and lead two, surely we can lead one between us," Nancy said. She thought of them leaving the Anchor while their parents were still asleep. We can leave a note, she thought. Otherwise Daddy might object.

Susan was coming back from her lunch now. "Oh thanks a million," she said looking at the cleaned tack. "Would one of you like to tack up Merlin. There's Professor Hunstein coming for private tuition."

Fiona picked up Merlin's saddle. "Do you think you will be able to teach him?" she asked. "I mean, he's terribly erudite."

"I'll do my best," Susan said.

The professor had grey hair and very red cheeks. He drove into the yard in a sports car.

"And where's Mrs. Manners?" he asked.

"In hospital," Alan said.

"I see," replied Professor Hunstein looking round the yard. "So there's no one to instruct me."

"There's Susan," replied Fiona. "She knows quite a lot."

"Have I got Merlin?"

Fiona nodded. "He's ready for you. Susan's just bringing him out."

"Fine, I'll hack him out then. I know my way. It will

make a pleasant change." Professor Hunstein crossed the yard and took Merlin from Susan.

"You know Angela's rule. She never lets anyone go out alone," June said. "Can't someone stop him?"

"It's Susan's job," replied Fiona.

"I don't know what to say."

"You are riding in the field," Susan said in a loud voice. "Angela doesn't like people going out alone."

"She won't mind me. We're old friends. I've been here a long time. I will be back in an hour, but if I'm more just make a note of it and add the extra to the bill," replied Professor Hunstein, mounting with an effort. "She really can't expect me to have a lesson from you, that would be asking too much."

"It is one of her rules, sir," shouted Alan.

But Professor Hunstein simply brushed the remark away with a wave of a hand, and rode out of the drive looking old-fashioned in bowler hat, long hacking jacket, breeches and brown boots.

"You shouldn't have let him go, Susan," shouted Alan. "You are in charge here. Goodness knows what Angela will say when she hears. You'll probably get the sack."

Susan looked at them all glaring at her. "I don't want to run the place," she shouted. "You can run it. I'm sick of the whole business anyway. It's dying, isn't it? You run it and good luck to you."

She ran towards the caravan swallowing tears, thinking I'll tell Mike what they said, how awful everything is. He'll know what to do. I can't go on like this, working day and night. I won't even have a day off, not as things are going . . .

"You shouldn't have said that," Fiona told Alan. "It was bad enough the professor being so rude to her, without you adding your little bit."

"She's so wet," Alan replied. "She has much more authority than we have. She could have said, 'I'm afraid

I have definite instructions from Mrs. Manners that you are not to go out alone.' "

"Perhaps she doesn't think quickly," June said.

"What will Angela say if she's not here when she comes back?" asked James. "I will go and see her. I might make her change her mind."

He ran past the lodge, where the curtains were drawn as though someone had died. He knocked on the door of the caravan.

"Who is it? Oh, come in," Susan said. She was sitting on one of the sofas which turned into beds smoking a cigarette.

"Who sent you?" she asked looking James up and down.

"I sent myself, Susan," replied James. "You can't give up. It wouldn't be fair to Mrs. Manners, her being sick. You must think again," he said, looking at a pile of hair curlers on a table. "Please Susan, stay till Angela comes back."

"I'll think about it," replied Susan. "In the meantime, this is my afternoon off, so skip it, scram, go!"

He ran back to the others still in the yard and told them what had happened. "We can manage without her anyway, so why worry. Angela will be able to save her wages if she leaves," Alan said.

"But she will need someone else for term time," replied Fiona.

"If the stables are still here then," June said.

"If she ever gets better," added James seeing a void which nothing would ever fill.

"We'll do afternoon stables. Come on, Nancy," said Naomi, fetching a wheelbarrow. "I think we had better leave for home after that. Mummy doesn't like us being late. She's afraid of nasty strangers on the bus."

She did not want to think beyond the moment. She fetched two pitchforks, a broom and a shovel.

"I'll go home and start on the banners," said Alan.

"See you tomorrow. I'm not much good at getting up, so I won't be among the first."

Fiona groomed Buccaneer and put on his tail bandage. James walked down the drive to look for Professor Hunstein and Merlin.

"Just like Alan to leave us the grooming," June told Fiona. "Shall I fill up the haynets?"

Moonstruck, Firefly and Buccaneer were normally stabled; but Seagull was still in so June filled him a haynet as well. He was standing listlessly in his box. He was too small to look over the door and was not interested in his hay, nor in the piece of bread June had in her hand. She stood talking to him for a long time and all the time her spirits were sinking and she kept thinking, everything's going wrong, supposing he doesn't get well? Supposing he dies, and we never get enough signatures? And the stables close down?

.   .   .   .   .

James was walking up the drive with Professor Hunstein. Merlin had slipped on the road and grazed his knees. But Professor Hunstein would not speak to James. He rode towards the stables with a fixed expression, ignoring him completely. And James thought, he's calling me an immigrant to himself, he's wishing I would go back to where I came from, which is here, because I was born here in this town; but one day I will be a great jockey. He will want racing tips from me then, but I shall ride past him with my head in the air. I shan't tell him anything. He looked at Merlin's knees and wondered what Angela would say if she could see them and he thought, everything's going wrong. We're no good at running the riding school, not even Alan and Fiona who I've always thought could run anything. He said, "How did he hurt his knees, sir?" and he made the "sir" very loud, but still Professor Hunstein made no reply, which reminded

James of his little sister, who sometimes sulked for hours, refusing to speak to anyone.

Naomi took Merlin from Professor Hunstein. She looked at his knees and said, "Oh Professor, how did it happen? Mrs. Manners will be upset."

And Professor Hunstein said, "It's hardly anything. All it needs is a little Dettol and water. I must go now. I've got an appointment," and got into his car and drove away.

"Heavens! what a beast," Fiona said. "He might have apologised." She bent down and looked at Merlin's broad grey knees. "There's grit in them," she said. "What a terrible day this has been. Does anyone know where Angela keeps the antiseptic?"

They bathed Merlin's knees and put kneecaps on him with cotton wool inside. They bedded down another box for him and saw that the sun was going down again. Naomi and Nancy went home and James and June and Fiona went round the boxes once more, checking the water buckets. The day seemed to have lasted for ever. June could hardly remember the morning. Fiona mounted her bike and rode away. Her mother was dishing up dinner when she reached home.

"Paul telephoned," she said. "I don't know why you're always out when he rings. He wanted you to go to the cinema with him. I expect he's taken someone else by now."

"I don't care about Paul," Fiona shouted. "He lectures me all the time and he's smug. I would much rather spend the evening with Buccaneer than go to the cinema with *him*. I don't know why he keeps ringing up. It's been a terrible day. Seagull's had colic, Angela is in hospital and idiotic Professor Hunstein let Merlin fall down on the road . . . and oh, I nearly forgot, Soppy Susan is sulking in her caravan demanding days off as though she worked in the post office." She collapsed in a chair. "I don't suppose we'll go to the Horse Trials either," she added.

"So all my schooling has been for nothing, though I suppose it will mean I'll get more when I sell Buccaneer, or Daddy will."

But her mother only said, "I wish you had gone to the cinema with Paul, darling. It would have taken your mind off the riding school. Angela Manners and Buccaneer are becoming an obsession with you."

"You don't care about Buccaneer at all, do you?" Fiona asked. "You never have. You want me to wear skirts and twin sets and go out with Paul."

"Well, it would be nice if you changed out of jodhs or jeans occasionally," her mother said.

. . . . .

June was home, walking up and down the living room which was strewn with toys. Rosie was sitting on a potty and the baby was sucking the corner of the tablecloth and dribbling. June felt sick. Tea had been left for her on the table. Her parents had gone out the minute she had appeared, leaving her in charge.

"We've been expecting you for the last hour," her mother had said, putting on her coat. "We won't be gone more than thirty minutes at the most." And June, who had intended telling her mother everything which had happened felt cheated. She knew her mother's thirty minutes which ran into hours. She went to the window and could see the stables beneath the setting sun and she started to worry about Seagull again.

. . . .

Naomi and Nancy found high tea waiting for them on the table in the living room. Their mother appeared from the lounge bar and kissed them both. "I thought you were never coming home," she said. "I was getting worried." She smelt of drink and was wearing high heels, a black

51

frock and earrings. "I've got you a nice tea," she continued. "I'm sure you must be hungry; when you've
finished chuck everything in the sink and watch telly."

"Angela Manners was taken to hospital," Naomi said.

"Oh dear, I'm sorry. Who is looking after the stables?"
her mother asked.

"We are," Nancy replied, sitting down at the table.

"Not just you, surely?"

"No, lots of us," Naomi answered and thought of
Merlin's grazed knees and wondered whether the knee
caps had slipped yet and whether they had done right to
keep him in. It's a terrible responsibility, she thought.

Nancy was imagining them catching Jasmine, The
Witch and Tomtit in the morning. Their field belonged to
a private house a mile from the stables. The house had
once owned twenty acres, but bit by bit, acre by acre it
had gone for building until only the field nearest the
house remained, surrounded by new houses on three sides.

"Bags I ride Tomtit and lead Jasmine," Nancy said.

"You can't bag. You know bagging's forbidden,"
shouted Naomi, growing red in the face. "We can each
lead Jasmine half the way; that's much fairer."

$\quad$ $\S$ $\quad$ $\S$ $\quad$ $\S$ $\quad$ $\S$ $\quad$ $\S$

James was home too, saying nothing, looking glum
and uncommunicative, so that his mother said, "What's
the matter, Jamie? What's gone wrong with your day,
eh?" and put her hand under his chin and looked into
his face. But he could only mutter "Nothing." He felt
physically bruised by the day, if that was possible. It
seemed to have lasted for ever without beginning or end.
I wish I could see Angela, he thought, but I'm not a
relation and I can't pretend I am. He was worrying about
Seagull, about Angela, about Merlin, about the way
Professor Hunstein had treated him.

"I feel ill," he said, sitting at the table with his head

52

in his hands. "Do you think we will save the stables, Mum? How much time is there left?"

"Not long," his mother answered. "Not according to what I've heard. They want the houses soon, real soon. Maybe we'll get one. You'd like to live there, wouldn't you? It would be a real lovely place to live. Think of it . . . we might have a real nice bathroom all to ourselves," she said, smiling her broadest smile, which was very broad indeed.

Alan had cut up three worn sheets. He hoped his mother would not mind. He set his poster paints out on his bedroom floor and lay on his stomach and painted SAVE THE RIDING SCHOOL in large red letters. He drew a horse's head underneath and painted it red too. Then he fetched another piece of sheet and painted DOWN WITH THE COUNCIL in blue. His parents were watching television in the next room. He had a desk of his own which was covered with packets of stamps. Piles of clothes lay in an untidy heap on a leather-seated chair. A photograph of himself on Firefly hung above his bed. It's got to do some good, he thought. We've got to win. If we lose I shall go away from here, I don't care what anyone says. I don't want to stay and watch the horses going. I shall run away to sea, I'm old enough.

Chapter Six

During the next three days they groomed and mucked out, taught and cleaned tack. Seagull recovered. Merlin's knees healed. Suddenly everything seemed better. Fiona rang up the hospital only to be told that Angela was under sedation and could not be visited. Naomi and Nancy brought Tomtit, Jasmine and The Witch from the bottom field each morning and took them back in the evenings. It was a wonderful feeling riding through the town with three horses. It was something they would never forget— the clip-clop of hoofs along the side streets, people rushing to the windows of terraced houses to look at them, the smell of the gasworks, the sun rising above the rooftops. It was engraved on their memories for ever. Nor would they forget the ride back in the evening with the sun going down, toddlers calling gee-gee as they passed; they felt suddenly as though they owned the whole town. "This is the life," Naomi said. "This, not the Anchor and the smell of beer and tobacco."

June was wishing that time would stand still. Her mother had found her great-uncle's address after a long search. He lived in London. "In one of the worst parts," Alan said, reading June's writing with a frown. Then Susan visited Angela and brought back a message for Fiona and Alan.

They read it together in the saddle room:—

"Dear Fiona and Alan,

I haven't put off the horsebox so you can go on Saturday. You are old enough to cope on your own now anyway. The box will call for you at eight thirty. Good luck,

Angela."

"She doesn't say anything about coming back," Fiona said.

"A good thing too. We don't want her back too soon. She might forbid the march," replied Alan.

"We'll be able to collect signatures at the Horse Trials after all," Fiona said.

"I'll go as your groom," June said.

"I will go as Alan's," James added quickly.

"We will stay behind and run the riding school with Susan, won't we, Nancy?" Naomi asked.

"If Susan doesn't take the week-end off. She has one in four, and it's ages since she had one," Fiona replied.

"I think I'll just run through the dressage test," Alan said. "I haven't even thought about it for days."

The banners were made. June's mother had stitched them on to bean poles provided by Fiona. There were two double ones, and six on one pole only, which looked like flags. James was to carry a double one with June. They were to be in front on Flotsam and Jetsam. Everyone was to wear a white shirt.

Fiona tacked up Buccaneer. It will be strange going without Angela, she thought. There will be no one to tell me how to ride the course, to comment on the dressage test. I wish Mummy and Daddy were horsy.

Alan was tacking up Firefly too; they rode towards Angela's arena together. They watched each other ride the dressage test. Fiona criticised Firefly's extended trot. "It lacks energy and impulsion," she yelled.

And Alan stopped and shouted back, "It doesn't. You don't know what you're talking about, you idiot."

And Fiona shouted, "All right, if you're going to be rude I won't look."

Then Alan told Fiona that her halt was useless, and Fiona said it wasn't and that he didn't know anything; and they both knew suddenly how much they were missing Angela. "I know I shan't do any good tomorrow. I haven't practised enough and I'm all on edge," Fiona said.

55

"Firefly hasn't had enough exercise. I'm going to take him out for a hack now—coming?" Alan asked and Fiona knew it was a peace offering.

"All right, but I hope Angela doesn't mind you hacking Firefly without her."

"Oh, for heaven's sake, I'm not a child," retorted Alan.

Fiona wanted to remind him of Professor Hunstein, but she refrained, for the day was too lovely to be marred by argument. They hacked down the track which wound past the new comprehensive school, rising classroom by classroom from the green turf, and beyond them, the woods lay dappled with sunlight. There was peace in the woods among the tall beech trees. Less flies buzzed round the horses' heads. The leaves on the trees were green, yellow and rust announcing the end of summer. Firefly and Buccaneer walked easily on loose reins. Alan made plans, his voice going on and on through the hot morning.

"We'll visit June's uncle the day after tomorrow. We'll have to pay our own fares somehow. I don't know how James will manage, but he must come, so must June," he said. "Then on Monday we will start practising for the march. We can go round and round the top meadow. I think I had better go in front of June and James after all. You can bring up the rear, keeping the people on their own ponies together. You can ride forward and take Firefly when I go up the steps to the Town Hall. We can rehearse that too in the top meadow."

"Supposing the ponies are afraid of the banners?" asked Fiona.

"We'll school them not to be. We've got a week," Alan replied.

They were out of the woods now in a lane. The banks on each side were white with cows' parsley.

"I wish we could ride like this for ever. That we never had to face up to reality," Fiona said.

The track passed on the far side of the new comprehensive school. They could see the riding school like

56

an island among the fields. Then Fiona gave a cry. "Look in the top field," she shouted. "There's a lorry dumping bricks in the top field." And all the peace of the morning vanished as they closed their legs on their horses' sides.

"So they've begun already!" Alan cried.

"We must padlock the gate," Fiona shouted. "We've got a padlock at home in the garden shed. I'll bring it

"There's a lorry dumping bricks in the top field"

after lunch. How could they do it while Angela was in hospital? It isn't fair. She'll never get well now." And all the time they were galloping. Alan turned to spit at the comprehensive school as he passed. His whole body seethed with anger.

"We'll throw the bricks over the gate," he shouted. "I don't care if I'm sent to prison for it."

"You wouldn't go to prison. You would go to an approved school," shouted Fiona, crouching over Buccaneer's withers, feeling dust in her eyes, watching the lather grow on his neck.

They could see June and James now running towards the bricks like ants.

"They are going to throw them out," shouted Fiona. "And it won't do any good." Buccaneer's long strides were eating up the ground, his hoofs thudding on the hard lane sounding like hammer against flint. And Fiona was hating the sunshine now. She wanted the heavens to break. She looked at the bricks and thought, they are the beginning of the end. They mean the council will never give in.

.   .   .   .   .

James and June carried the bricks carefully through the gate which they had opened, dumping each one gently, as if it was an egg, under the council's notice at the top of the drive. They hardly spoke to one another. After a time their hands began to feel sore and June could feel sweat trickling down her face. Then Fiona appeared looking hot and angry.

"I'm riding Buccaneer home to get a padlock," she cried. "Keep at it."

James looked at the bricks. "We must be half way through, June," he said.

"I hope Mum doesn't look out of the window and see me," June replied. "She might be very angry."

"We've only broken one brick so far and they look quite tidy here," replied James.

Fiona reached home. Sweat dripped off Buccaneer's sides. She tied him to the garden gate and found the padlock and a chain quite easily on her father's work bench. Her mother called to her from an upstairs window.

"What's the matter, darling? Have you forgotten something?"

"No, I just came for the padlock. They are putting bricks in the top field now," Fiona shouted, mounting with the padlock and chain in one hand. She trotted through the town and someone shouted "Cowboy!" She could hardly wait for the traffic lights to change at the top of the street. She was nearly as hot as Buccaneer now. When she reached the drive, James and June were moving the last few bricks and another brick lorry was parking by the notice. A man in overalls climbed out of the cab and stood staring at June and James.

"What's the game?" he asked. "I put those in the field, didn't I?"

Naomi, Nancy and Alan were running down the drive towards them. Fiona dismounted and padlocked the gate.

"That field doesn't belong to the council yet," she said. "They have no right to put bricks in it."

The man was tall and wore a cap, boiler suit and working boots.

"I don't know anything about that. But I do know my orders and here they are," he replied taking a scrap of paper from his pocket. *"Unload lorry through gate on right of notice board"*, he read aloud. "Clear as crystal ain't it?"

"It may be clear, but it's wrong," replied Alan, suddenly beside them. "There's still a petition to be delivered and a public inquiry to be held."

The lorry's engine was still running. The driver switched it off and lit himself a cigarette. He offered one to Alan, who took it though he hardly ever smoked. Everybody stood looking at the brick lorry. "Bit of an impasse, isn't it?" asked the driver after a time. "Is there a phone at the stables?"

"In the lodge," replied Fiona doubtfully.

"Can I use it?" The driver was already walking towards his lorry. The day was unbearably hot. Alan said, "I'll go with you," and climbed into the cab. The lorry made a hissing noise as it disappeared along the drive.

"Well, we've won. He hasn't put them in the field," June said.

"But how will we stop the bulldozers?" asked Fiona. She led Buccaneer along the drive. Steam rose from his sides and evaporated in the hot air.

"We are losing, aren't we?" Naomi asked. "They are going to win."

"Not if June's uncle can help," replied Fiona briskly,

59

wondering if she really believed her own words. "He can speak to the government. They can overrule anyone—even the council."

They could see the lorry driver coming out of the lodge now. He ground the end of his cigarette into the gravel with his heel.

"Seems you've won for the time being," he said. "I'm to dump the bricks where you put them others."

They felt a great surge of cautious joy. June looked at her sore hands. James straightened his back and smiled. Naomi and Nancy both started to whistle at the same moment—they often did things at the same moment being twins. Fiona said, "That's something. It's a bit much seeing bricks dumped by the council on private land."

"It's only till they've consulted their solicitor," replied the driver, climbing into his lorry. "Well, bye-bye."

"He was nice, wasn't he? I mean he could have been absolutely horrible," Naomi said.

"Our campaign hasn't really got going yet. My letter will be in the paper tomorrow with luck," Alan said.

The class was coming in from the paddock now and there was not a cloud in the sky and it seemed impossible to believe that quite soon the stables might be gone, the fields too, even the trees.

Susan was hot and red in the face. The children in the class were arguing with her, saying, "Angela never said that," and "How do you know? You are only a working pupil." And Susan, looking round the yard, thought, I don't care if it does all go. Let people live here.

June said, "I must go. I promised Mum I would help her today, because tomorrow I shall be out all day." She ran along the drive and now there was a tremendous stack of bricks, red and new under the notice board. It made her heart give a silly leap when she saw them, and she was suddenly certain that the council would never take them away; even if the riding school won they would remain there for ever. I don't want to grow older, she thought. I don't want to have to keep a house clean and wash clothes. I want to go on being as I am, only richer with my own pony, and to be able to buy things for Mum. To stop her being so tired all the time—an electric cleaner, a fridge, an automatic washing machine.

*   *   *   *   *

"What did the lorry driver want?" Susan asked.

"To put bricks in Angela's field of all the cheek," replied Naomi. They were cleaning tack in the saddle room. Fiona had taken hers completely to pieces. Alan had vanished on some pretext or other. James kept asking the time. His father had promised to take him to a football match. He had never been to one before. The gravel was burning hot outside. It will be hot on the pitch, he thought. I hope Dad keeps out of the fights.

He went at last, shouting over his shoulder, "I will see you tomorrow then, Fiona. I will be here by six, or maybe earlier, maybe five, maybe four. I don't know, Fiona, early anyway." He thought of Angela clean and washed in the hospital. She must come home soon, he decided, because she wasn't so bad, just overworked and upset.

Some boys were climbing on the bricks. They said something rude, but he pretended not to hear. The town smelt of petrol and carbon dioxide. The basement looked greyer in the sunlight. He could see the cracks in the walls.

"Hurry Jamie boy," shouted his mother, as he ran down the steps. "Your father's waiting and you've had no dinner."

He pulled off his shirt and went straight to the sink to wash and all the time he was thinking of the wonderful moment when Angela came back.

*   *   *   *   *

Fiona stayed till the evening. She washed Buccaneer's tail and bandaged it. She spent hours with the body brush and finished him off with the rubber. She mucked out his box and spread it with threequarters of a bale of clean straw. She put his rug on and bandaged his legs. She filled up his water bucket and fed him and went home on her bicycle without looking at the bricks by the notice board. But though she did not look she could not forget they were there, and it spoilt everything. I don't really care how I do tomorrow, she thought, wheeling her bike into the garage. It seems irrelevant somehow. I don't think Alan cares either. I've never been to any show before without Angela. She won't be there to walk round the course with us or to tell us where we've gone wrong in the dressage.

Her parents were out. She fried herself bacon and eggs in the kitchen. Then she started to work on her clothes. Her boots were filthy, her coat was missing a button. She pricked her finger and it bled onto her cream-coloured breeches and suddenly she wanted to scream, why does everything have to go wrong? Why can't life be perfect? She took her breeches to the sink and washed the blood off and she kept seeing the bricks heaped by the notice, waiting to take over the fields.

. . . . .

"I hope Angela will let us go on fetching Tomtit and co.," Naomi said when they had turned the three ponies into their field and stood watching them roll on the hot, dusty earth by the field gate.

"I feel a much better rider. I think I will be able to take C test in the spring," Nancy said. "But will Angela come back, do you think? I mean supposing she's really ill? She could have a tumour on the brain like Cousin Alec."

"Oh shut up, don't be so morbid," replied Naomi. "Of course she's coming back. I'll beat you to the road."

When they reached the road they decided to walk the whole way home. Their shoes were dusty; they had head-collars over their shoulders and crash caps on their heads.

"I feel marvellously different from everyone else," Naomi said, looking at the hairs from Tomtit which had stuck to her jodhpurs.

"I wish we could do this every day," Nancy answered. "I'm sick of buses and people."

Their father met them in the kitchen. "You didn't walk through the streets like that?" he asked. "In those dirty shoes?"

But they only laughed. "Oh Daddy," Naomi cried. "You are mad. What does it matter?"

"We had a lovely day. I led Jasmine all the way to the field. It was super, Daddy," shouted Nancy.

Meanwhile James watched the football match. He cheered when his father cheered and clapped and shouted, but his mind was not really there at all, for he kept thinking of Angela coming back, wishing that the last ten days could have been nothing but a dream. He was nearly crushed when they left the stadium, so dense was the crowd. He held onto his father's coat, and his father was very tall and they survived with only three buttons lost off James's shirt and a foot bruised by a hobnail boot.

"Well, how was it?" his father asked when they were outside in the street, walking homewards as the street lights came on.

"Okay," James answered. "But not as good as a horse show. You can't beat a horse show."

⁊   ⁊   ⁊   ⁊   ⁊

Boning his boots, Alan was working out a programme for tomorrow. Get up at six, he decided, eat breakfast, reach stables by seven, groom. Susan can do the mucking out and the plaiting. I must not forget the petition. He felt on edge now and doubted whether he would sleep at all.

63

I haven't looked up the trains to London yet, he thought, and we haven't even started practising the march. Time seemed to be running out; and for Alan there was never enough time. It was the same at school; there was never time to join all the societies and clubs, to play football and run cross country. He put his boots away and it was ten o'clock now. His mother called, "Bed, darling. Hurry up now. You've got a busy day tomorrow."

As if I didn't know, thought Alan, and hoped there would not be a drop fence. I shall never be ready, he thought frantically. Where have I put the dressage test? I must run through it again.

"Have you seen my dressage test?" he shouted,

"What did you say?" called his mother.

"I said, where's the dressage test," bawled Alan and he could feel the pressure mounting, time passing. "I've lost my dressage test," he shouted again. "And I can't find any clean socks for tomorrow."

Chapter Seven

Fiona arrived first at the riding school. It was five o'clock and the moonlight was fading from the sky. There were no lights on anywhere and Buccaneer was still lying down in his box. Fiona loved the early morning. It was suddenly as though everything was hers—the streets, the houses and even the people asleep inside. She was wearing an old pair of jeans, a polo-necked sweater and Wellington boots.

Quite soon afterwards Naomi and Nancy arrived with Tomtit, Jasmine and The Witch from the bottom field. Dawn had come by this time and the sun was breaking through a veil of clouds.

"It's lovely being so early," Naomi said, dismounting. "The streets were completely empty. We felt like burglars, didn't we, Nancy?"

Nancy nodded. "It was like living years ago without the cars—it was fabulous," she said.

. . . . .

James was running up the steps of the basement. He ran along the street silently in plimsolls. Even so a policeman stopped him, stepping suddenly from a doorway.

"Where are you going, son?" he asked. "Not running away, are you?"

And James had to explain everything—about the Horse Trials, about the riding school, about Angela being ill, before he was allowed to go on. It was not the first time he had been stopped by the police. Whenever a child was suspected of any offence, James was stopped. As he ran on he could feel anger rising inside himself. By the time he reached the notice board he wanted to pick up the bricks and smash them one by one to get quits with the policeman and pay back the council for spoiling his life. But he kept control of himself and when he reached the stableyard his anger evaporated. Buccaneer's mane was already plaited. Fiona was going home to change.

.　　.　　.　　.　　.

"You can't go yet, June," shouted her mother. "Not till you've had a proper breakfast."

"But I must," shouted June. "I'm late," and ran down the stairs three at a time pulling on her coat. The sunlight hit her in the eyes when she stepped outside. "If I had stayed another minute I would never have got away, she decided, already seeing the bricks stacked by the notice board.

She met Alan hurrying towards the riding school as well. He held out a newspaper. "Have you seen this?" he cried. "Look, my letter is in. They've printed it!"

"Oh good, how super," June replied, running on towards the riding school, thinking, I promised to help Fiona and I'm late, terribly late.

"You haven't looked," shouted Alan furiously, thinking, twit, silly idiot, ill-educated twit.

He had shown it to his parents when they emerged from their bedroom looking for the post and wishing for cups of tea. A councillor had been asked by the editor to reply. It was reprinted below Alan's letter. Alan knew it by heart already. It said that the character of the area had been changing for some time, that riding schools should not be inside the perimeter of a town, that no resident living in the vicinity had asked for consultation and that most of them were delighted with the plan. It said that Alan— "Mr. Alan Thornly"—'is catering for a small minority

66

whereas the council is attending to the needs of the vast majority of the population'.

He showed the paper to everyone when he reached the stables. Susan had plaited Firefly. Now she was mucking out. There were five minutes to spare before the horsebox arrived. James could not read much of the letter, but he said, "Very nice, Alan, a very nice letter, real nice. It makes you look important too, Alan," and realised that he had forgotten to bring any food for lunch and had only a few pennies in his pocket.

Naomi and Nancy were grooming the ponies for the ten o'clock class. "It's fabulous," they cried politely in unison. And now the horsebox was coming up the drive, and it was too late for James to go home and find something for lunch. June put a head-collar on Buccaneer. James picked up a bag of feed and two haynets full of hay.

The driver stopped the horsebox. "How is Mrs. Manners?" he asked, getting out. "I heard she was poorly."

Ten minutes later Firefly and Buccaneer were boxed. Fiona arrived hot and flustered. "Everything went wrong," she said. "Mummy made me have a cooked breakfast. Your letter looks marvellous, Alan. Daddy was madly impressed."

Nothing seemed real without Angela. Even the driver looked uneasy. "We had better be off, then," he said. "I don't know how long *she* thought it would take."

The roads were full of cars making for the coast. June and James had insisted on riding in the groom's compartment. Alan and Fiona sat with the driver, discussing the end of the riding school. But it's not going to end, Fiona thought like a drowning person trying to catch hold of driftwood. We are going to win.

"It's a shame," the driver continued. "She had built up a nice business, hadn't she? But that's life nowadays, isn't it? I've got a mate who's lost his whole house in a road widening scheme, properly cut up he was about it. But what can you do?"

"Fight," Alan replied. "I've got a petition here, You'll sign it, won't you?"

"It won't do any good, but I'll sign it of course," the driver said.

They were late arriving. Horses were already in the collecting ring for the dressage test. The driver let down the ramp and they led Firefly and Buccaneer out of the box and peeled off their bandages.

"Don't forget the petition. There's pen and paper in the cab," Alan said, mounting with the sun in his eyes, memorising the dressage test as he rode Firefly towards the collecting ring.

"Get our numbers, June," shouted Fiona. "Hurry!"

They were missing Angela all the time now. Fiona would have given anything to hear her say, "Keep calm. There's lots of time. You can go in last."

Firefly was dancing and hopping instead of trotting at a balanced extended trot. Alan forgot his letter; he started to ride a circle and noticed that Firefly's drop noseband was too tight. I'm going to make a mess of it, he thought dismounting. I shan't get him to walk on a loose rein, or to stand still when I take off my hat; and he could feel panic rising inside him, making his heart beat faster and his legs feel like jelly.

But now James was running towards him, looking small and dark-skinned in a very white shirt and jeans. He was waving a number and shouting, "Three more horses to go. You follow Fiona." And suddenly Alan seemed to have reached reality at last and could remember the test perfectly.

Five minutes later Fiona was entering the dressage arena, while June watched, clutching a stable rubber in one hand.

Alan did not look. He rode away, thinking, I won't be better than her anyway, I never am.

68

Fiona rode in and bowed and now she was not missing Angela any more. She felt completely alone and in control of the situation and Buccaneer was going marvellously. He dropped his nose and halted, standing perfectly with his hocks under him and Fiona thought, everything is going to be all right.

Standing at the ring ropes June thought, that was fantastic. I wish I could get Seagull to halt like that. But James was not watching. He had fetched a petition and was asking a man with a shooting stick to sign.

"Is this in support of coloureds?" the man asked. "Because I'm not going to sign anything like that. I think you should all go home to where you belong. You are creating slums and filling up the schools. It's a disgrace." And suddenly James felt like crying. It's always the same, he thought. They always think we shouldn't be here. "I'm going to the West Indies when I'm older," he said, but the man was walking away now, swinging his shooting stick and muttering, "Of all the damned cheek," and James was afraid to ask anyone else.

Fiona was leaving the ring now. She knew she had ridden a good test, but she wished Angela was there to confirm it. She shouted, "Good luck, Alan," as he rode in, looking tall and tense on Firefly.

"That was fabulous," June said. "I wish I could ride like you."

"You will be able to soon. I'm not really very good. I did a lousy serpentine," Fiona replied, before she remembered that nothing goes on for ever and that time was running out. "Can you get me a petition?" she said then, and completely forgot Alan, crossing the arena at an extended trot.

June held Buccaneer while Fiona approached the ringside cars with the petition and saw Alan saluting the judge for the last time before riding out of the ring on a loose rein.

"It wasn't as good as yours," he shouted. "At least I

69

don't think so, but it was the best I've ever done." And now suddenly anything seemed possible . . . Badminton, competing at the Olympic Games for England, anything . . .

Everyone was signing Fiona's petition. They said things like, "Of course. Everything good is being destroyed," and "Soon there will be no fields left," and "Thank good-

Buccaneer was going marvellously

ness you are fighting. Demand a public enquiry. Write to your M.P. Make a gigantic fuss."

When Fiona returned to June she had collected fifty signatures and Alan took the sheet of paper and said, "I'll carry on." Buccaneer and Firefly were tied up now and there were only two competitors left to ride the dressage test.

"I wonder what Angela is doing now," June said to James.

"Resting, having a real good rest, June," James replied

and imagined her propped up with pillows in a very clean white bed.

"I wish she would come back. Do you think she knows about the bricks? I wish we could visit her," June said.

"I don't know," James replied. "Mum thinks she's having lots of pills, tranquillisers she says, something to quieten her down."

He felt sad now, as though he was buried or trapped in a tunnel without an end, as though nothing would ever get any better. "Mum wants new flats," he said.

"So does mine," June replied. "It's awful, isn't it?"

June shared her lunch with James and then it was time to tack up the horses for the cross country.

Alan had collected another ninety signatures. "No one refused," he said, hastily swallowing egg sandwiches. "Not a single person."

James led Firefly up and down waiting for him. He wished he was like Alan, with a nice house, an important father and a letter published in the local paper.

"I can't mount yet," Alan said. "I haven't walked the course." He walked the course with Fiona.

"I don't know how I shall jump that timber wagon at the bottom of the hill," Fiona said.

"I'm going to trot; otherwise Firefly will get right under it and then I'm finished," replied Alan.

"The drop fence looks enormous," continued Fiona.

"I shall take that slowly too," answered Alan.

He was not afraid at all, only calm and longing to be jumping the course already; whereas Fiona was biting her nails and had a pain in the pit of her stomach, and was wanting advice desperately on how to jump each fence. Horses were being tacked up when they returned to the horsebox. June was working on Buccaneer with the rubber. James was trying to calm Firefly, who was sweating again; and the weather had changed; the sky was full of ominous clouds racing across the blue to join one another in a vast grey blanket which could only be herald-

71

ing a storm. People picked up picnic things and put rugs into cars. The first competitor started the cross country course.

"We had better mount," Alan said. He had left his mackintosh at home and was regretting it now.

"I bet it's pouring when I go round," said Fiona pessimistically. "The track through the wood to the timber wagon will be like murder by then."

"Number Two has just started," replied Alan, pulling up Firefly's girths.

"You haven't had any lunch, Fiona," said June. "I'm sure you should eat something."

"I had a cooked breakfast, that's enough to keep me going all day," replied Fiona.

Buccaneer was fresh. He kept looking around as though he expected to see hounds on the horizon. The third competitor was just starting now; the first one was home, dismounting from his steaming horse, saying, "I refused at the bullfinch and he stopped twice at the drop fence. I'm out of it now." He looked older than her and ex- perienced and suddenly Fiona wished that she had never come, that she was at home, reading a book on her bed, or having lunch with her mother on a high stool in the kitchen, which was what they often did, when her father was away.

But it was too late now, her number was being called; drops of rain were falling from the leaden sky. The first rumble of thunder seemed to shake the earth as she rode towards the collecting ring steward. He was a young man in a cap. "Not yet, don't go yet," he said, "Wait till I drop the flag. Are your girths tight? Good luck." And suddenly she was galloping across the grass, and every- thing was forgotten except the course. Buccaneer was going steadily as though he knew he had to go a long way, and the first jump was easy, just a simple rail fence. As they landed on the other side, Fiona thought, everything is going to be all right. The next fence was easy too; but

72

the drop fence seemed to go on for ever, and then they were in the wood and the rain was driving at them and Fiona could hardly see the loaded timber wagon, solid with a tree, at the bottom of the track.

She tried to check Buccaneer and he put in a short stride and scraped the top; but they were over, galloping uphill towards the bank with the fence on top with the wind behind them.

Buccaneer had taken over now. He had been born in Ireland and he knew how to manage the bank; two minutes later and with three more fences behind them, they were approaching the coffin and Alan had started the course, crouched over Firefly's neck like a jockey.

The bullfinch was easy. Another minute and Buccaneer was slithering down the pit and over the jump at the bottom; he took the pond jump in his stride too, and now there was only one jump left and the wind was still behind them. Galloping towards it Fiona thought, I shall always remember this whatever else happens, even if I never ride again. Buccaneer lengthened his stride and then they were over the last fence and nearly back with the horseboxes and the crowd, and June jumping up and down and shouting, "You've jumped a clear round. You're in the lead, you must be."

Firefly was going too fast. He nearly fell at the timber wagon. He rapped the rail on the bank so hard that Alan heard the wood crack. He could not turn him for the bullfinch and had to go back. He raced down the pit and only just got over the fence at the bottom; there was an enormous flash of lightning which seemed to light the whole sky as he raced towards the pond jump, so that for a second the water looked on fire. But he cleared that too and suddenly the worst was behind them and Alan felt a great rush of joy as they galloped towards the last

73

jump, and the sky started to clear and he could see the horseboxes in the distance and Fiona leading Buccaneer up and down.

I got round anyway, decided Alan. And it was an enormous course. Perhaps one day I really will ride at Badminton, or jump for England, who knows? I'm not

He took the pond jump in his stride too

giving up anyway, even if Angela goes, not now, not when I've got this far.

Firefly's neck was lathered with sweat. His sides were going in and out like bellows and sweat dripped from his stomach; but they had finished. Alan dismounted and his legs felt weak as though he had been in the saddle all day instead of a mere eight minutes.

"You were wonderful," said Fiona. "The fastest round yet."

"But I ran out. I had to go back. I shall lose some points there. And my dressage was not up to much," Alan answered.

"It was terriffic, Alan," James said. "He went like lightning." He led Firefly up and down, looking small and dark, and he thought, they are managing all right without Angela. They are the sort of people who can always get what they want, but what about me and June? We haven't important parents, or money; we are on our own.

"There's still the show jumping," Fiona said. "Buccaneer will probably hit everything," but already she could hear someone saying, "That girl over there is leading. She did a marvellous round; and she's lying second in the dressage."

And someone else chipped in to say, "Who is she?"

And no one seemed to know. Fiona ate her sandwiches in the horsebox. There seemed much more at stake now that she knew she was within reach of a prize. June had fed Buccaneer and the sun was shining again. Alan was counting the signatures on the petition.

"If you win, you will have your photograph in *Horse and Hound*, then we'll both have been in newspapers," he said. And Fiona thought, I don't care about that. I should probably look awful anyway. To win is enough for me.

Chapter Eight

Fiona had walked the course. Her name with Buccaneer was at the top of the score mark. She was leading with seven less penalties than her nearest rival. And it was her first real Horse Trials. It was almost impossible to believe. Alan was lying fifth. The open class was going round the cross-country course and already there seemed a whisper of evening in the air.

June was leading Buccaneer up and down. The first competitor was already in the collecting ring. Fiona pulled up her girths and mounted. "Good luck," June let go of the reins.

"I shall need it," Fiona replied.

"Even if you hit a fence you'll still be first," June answered.

"Supposing I refuse three times?"

"You won't."

Buccaneer was as sound as a bell. He wasn't even tired. The course wasn't big. There was one difficult combination; the rest was easy.

"Good luck," shouted James. "Go carefully, Fiona."

She rode into the ring and waited for the starting bell. When it went Buccaneer was ready. He approached each fence exactly right as though he had been jumping all his life. He took the gate, the wall and the parallel bars in his stride. He put in one stride between each fence in the combination and then there were only the hog's back and the water jump left, and it was as though she could smell victory in the air now and she kept thinking, if only Mummy and Daddy were here, or Angela, just someone to be pleased. Buccaneer cleared the hog's back and raced for the water. Fiona could hear the clapping before they landed and someone shouting, "Well done, Fiona, well done."

Photographers were photographing her as she rode out of the ring, and she thought, this should be the greatest moment of my life but it isn't, because instead of it being the beginning it may be the first and last Horse Trials I shall ever ride in. She dismounted and led Buccaneer to the horsebox while James and June ran beside her shrieking, "Jolly good, Fiona. It was smashing," and, "You've won, Fiona, you've won."

She gave Buccaneer a handful of oats. Alan was in the ring now. Firefly had knocked down the middle fence in the combination. Alan was trying to steady him. I shall never beat Fiona, he thought, but I am going to get round whatever happens. Firefly took the hog's back fast, putting in a short stride, and rapping the top pole; but it did not fall, and now there was only the water jump left, and he let Firefly have his head. They cleared the water jump flat out and suddenly it was all over . . . everything, the whole Horse Trials for him. It was fantastic, he decided, riding from the ring, but Firefly is not my horse and when Angela goes he will go too.

A lady in a tweed coat and skirt was talking to Fiona.

"I wondered whether you might like to compete at Colesbrook next spring," she said. "We are only inviting twenty people and we want to choose riders from them to train for the junior team."

"But I may not still have Buccaneer. I don't know what may have happened," replied Fiona.

"Are you selling him then? How much do you want for him?" The woman's eyes had lit up. "A thousand?" she asked.

"I don't know," Fiona replied. "I was only thinking of three hundred and fifty."

"That's ridiculous," the woman said. "Supposing you let me have your address and I will send you details of Colesbrook anyway and if you *do* want to sell him, be sure and let me know."

"That's ridiculous," the woman said

June stood on a bucket and undid Buccaneer's girths. She had heard the whole conversation and suddenly she wanted to cry. James was not saying anything. He helped Alan untack Firefly and all the time he was thinking, she can't sell Buccaneer, not now, not when they've gone so well together and she might compete for England . . . Alan had disappeared with the petition. The last competitor was going round the show jumping course and he knew that Fiona had won. They don't want me to be looked at for the team, he thought, and I shall never have another chance if Angela gives up. Suddenly he was running from car to car, saying, "Will you sign this petition? It's to save a first-class riding school," and all the time he was seeing Firefly going to another home with Angela's other horses.

    .   .   .   .   .

Fiona had been awarded her prize—a challenge cup and ten pounds. They had stuck the enormous rosette in the window of the horsebox and Alan's green one was there too.

"Mrs. Manners *will* be pleased," said the horsebox driver. "I never thought either of you would come in first."

Dusk had come already. Alan sat counting the names on the petition. "We've only got three hundred and fifty," he said.

"Give me one, I'll get my mates to sign," replied the driver.

"We're going to London tomorrow and we haven't looked up the trains yet," Fiona said.

"I'll look them up tonight. We had better assemble at the stables by about ten," Alan replied. "I'll pay for James's fare, if he hasn't any money."

"What about June? She's just as important. He's her uncle," Fiona asked.

"You'll have to help her," replied Alan.

The roads were full of people rushing to pubs or coming back from the coast. Street lights were on in towns. In the groom's department June said, "They will put street lights in the stable yard. I shall look at them and remember the ponies. Mum says I can ride beach ponies. She doesn't understand."

"They won't because we are going to win. What's your uncle like, June?" asked James.

"I don't know. He's old. He must be, because he was the last time I saw him and I was two then. I only hope he lives in the same place. It will be awful if we go all that way for nothing," June said. "Alan will be furious."

"Don't worry, June," replied James.

"I can't help it. I worry about everything. Mum says I'm made that way."

"Perhaps Angela will come home tomorrow. She's been away a long time, hasn't she, June?" asked James.

"Yes." June was sleepy now. She did not want to think about tomorrow. "I haven't any money for the fare," she muttered. "I shall have to ask Mum again. And I don't suppose Mum will have much either, because she bought Rosie a coat yesterday."

"I don't know what I shall do either. I may not go at all, June," James said. "Dad likes me to stay home Sundays . . ."

"I don't know how we get there when we reach London," continued June. "I haven't been for years and he may have moved."

:   :   :   :   :

Naomi and Nancy were waiting for them in the yard. Susan had gone out with Mike. Dusk had come quickly and Naomi and Nancy seemed to have been waiting for ever. But when the horsebox drew up at last with the two rosettes in the cab window everything seemed worthwhile.

"Jolly good," they shouted. "Who won the red?" They were more tired than they had ever been before. Their limbs felt limp with exhaustion; their arms ached from mucking out and grooming.

Fiona jumped out. She was spattered all over with mud. "I won," she said. "Buccaneer went like a dream. They want me to be considered for the junior team; but what's the good now?"

The driver was letting down the ramp. "Their loose boxes are ready," Nancy said. "Don't you think the place looks tidy? We've been working ever since you left. Susan packed up hours ago. She was in one of her moods."

Buccaneer was tucked up and looked as though he had been hunting all day. Firefly came down the ramp with a rush.

"We've got nearly five hundred signatures all told," Alan said. "We've had a field day."

Ten minutes later they were all going home. The street lights were on. They had agreed to meet next day at ten o'clock.

"I never thought she would win," Nancy said.

James was running. It was long past his tea time. He had never been out so late before all alone. He knew his mother would be waiting for him, looking up and down the street as she always did when he was late.

And I've got to go out tomorrow, he remembered. Alan says I can't let them down. But will Dad let me go and where's the money coming from for the train? Sometimes I wish it was all over, he thought suddenly, Angela, the lot—that I could forget or pretend it never happened, that she was never here.

　　　※　　　※　　　※　　　※　　　※

June was home already, drinking hot, sugary tea, saying over and over again, "She won, Mum. She did really. They may choose her for the team."

Fiona rushed into the manor house waving her rosette. "We won," she shouted. "Mummy, we won."

But it was her father who appeared first. "You're very late. We were getting quite worried," he said.

"Look, I won," she cried. "I won first prize. Buccaneer is worth a thousand pounds now. I may be chosen to represent England . . ."

It did not sound like life, it sounded too perfect, but the feeling of triumph was still with her. Nothing succeeds like success, she thought, while her parents' faces broke into smiles and her mother asked, "Did you say you had won?"

She nodded. "Buccaneer was marvellous," she said. "He knew how to jump the bank. He carried me round. I never knew he was so marvellous."

"Did you say he was worth a thousand pounds? That would buy a lot of shares," her father said.

"Or six months in Paris," suggested her mother.

"I don't want shares and I don't want Paris. I want Buccaneer," Fiona replied quickly. "He's the only thing I really want."

"But if Angela gives up?" asked her father.

"I shall kill myself. I'm not getting rid of Buccaneer, not for anything. Don't you want me to jump for England?" shouted Fiona. "Aren't you pleased."

* * * * *

"Don't ever stay out so late again." The twins were home.

"We couldn't leave before. We were in charge. Susan went on strike," Nancy replied.

Their mother had come out of the bar to greet them. "We thought you had been murdered. Daddy wanted to ring up the police," she said. "You could have telephoned. I hope you will stay at home tomorrow. We never see anything of you now."

"Someone has to do the work. Fiona and Alan were at the Horse Trials," Nancy explained. "Fiona won first prize."

"Supper is in the oven. I'm sorry, darlings, I must go back to the customers now," replied their mother. "I'll tell Daddy you are back."

"She won't want us to go tomorrow," Nancy said. "Today was super, wasn't it? I never knew I could do so much. I'm nearly as quick as Susan at mucking out now."

They smelt of horse. They washed their hands and ate supper and talked endlessly about the riding school, about the ponies and which got dirtiest and which had the best head. "I'm going to run a riding school when I'm grown up," Nancy said.

"I shall breed ponies and break them in," Naomi replied.

*   *   *   *   *

Alan was home now. His parents had gone out again; leaving a notice which read, GONE TO THE NEW INN. BACK SOON. There was supper waiting for him on the kitchen table—veal and ham pie, a salad, baked beans, apple pie. He took the petition to his bedroom. His mother had made his bed; but his jeans still lay in a crumpled heap on the floor where he had left them the day before. The banners stood in one corner of the room. His father had pinned a note to the one which said DOWN WITH THE COUNCIL. The note asked, "Isn't this rather rude?" They were a great family for notes. Once Alan's parents had quarrelled. Everything had been written on notes then. Alan had spent his time running from one to the other with scraps of paper. He had been eight then, and his love of horses had started then, perhaps as an escape, from the situation at home. Now he was envious of Fiona. I shall have to join the army if I'm to go on riding, he thought. I can be in the Queen's escort. And he saw himself in plumed helmet riding down the Mall on a black horse. I might like the army, he thought, it would be better than sitting in an office all day.

He ate his supper and then he rang up the railway station to find the time of a train to London in the morning.

"Ten forty-five is the first one," said the voice at the other end.

He counted his money after that; he had eighteen shillings and he knew it was too little for himself and James. I shall have to ask my mother, he thought. And she will say, "I only gave you fifteen shillings last week, Alan. Where does it all go?"

He looked at himself in the mirror above the chimney-piece and he liked what he saw—dark hair, firm chin, straight nose, steady grey-blue eyes. . . . I should look all right in a helmet with a sword at my side, he thought, and Fiona will never be able to be the same, because she's a girl.

He put his dirty plates in the sink and started to count the signatures on the petitions again which had increased to seven hundred and fifty altogether. And now his parents were home, coming through the door laughing, smelling of drink.

"I say, old boy," his father called. "Don't you think your banners are a bit rude? I mean, I've got friends on the Council. Did you see my note?"

He roughed Alan's hair in the way he hated. And his mother laughed and said, "You'll all be put in prison for insulting behaviour."

And neither of them asked about the Horse Trials. Alan put his rosette in his desk and went to bed. He could hear the owls hooting outside, and the street lights were on and all over the town people were going home to bed. Alan saw himself jumping for England in uniform, then he saw the march winding through the town two by two, and he thought, I'm not going to alter the banner. I hate the Council. I shall be leading the march, he thought and gradually as he dropped off to sleep, he saw himself walking up the steps of the Town Hall and now he was in full dress uniform, taking off his helmet and kneeling on the cold stone and his thoughts had become dreams.

.   .   .   .   .

Next day the weather was perfect. Susan greeted everyone by saying, "We've got to make the place look tidy. Angela is being allowed out for a couple of hours this afternoon."

"You make it sound as though she's in prison," Fiona replied.

"We won't be here," replied Alan, who had managed to borrow a pound from his mother.

"I wish I could be," said James, who had slunk out of home while the rest of the family slept. "Couldn't I stay, Alan?"

Alan shook his head. "You are very important to us," he replied. "That's why I am prepared to pay for your fare."

The twins had not arrived, but June was coming down the drive, her hair uncombed, looking as though she had been pulled through a hedge backwards.

"I had an awful job to get away and I had to break into Rosie's money box and I don't know how I shall ever pay her back," she said. Her face looked wan. "The others are getting whooping cough. They coughed all night," she continued. "Luckily I've had it."

Fiona turned Buccaneer into the top meadow. She watched him roll. "He's worth a thousand pounds," she said. "Isn't it fantastic?"

"Are we all here? It's time we went to the station," Alan announced. "Have you got your uncle's address, June?"

June gave him a creased piece of paper. "He's my great-uncle," she said. She felt nervous now. Supposing he's awful? she thought, without any teeth, and dirty? They'll

85

despise me for ever then. But one can't help one's relations.

"Where are you going?" cried Susan as they started to walk away down the drive. "Aren't you going to help? I can't manage on my own."

"To London," shouted Alan, and suddenly they were all running.

"We've only got ten minutes," Fiona said, "And we've got to get the tickets."

"What about Nancy and Naomi?" asked June. "Weren't they coming?"

"They were but they haven't. It's nearly twenty-five to eleven and they were supposed to be here by ten," replied Alan.

"I expect they are having parent troubles," suggested Fiona.

The train was in when they reached the station. Alan bought the tickets.

"I would much rather pay for myself, Alan," James said in a strained voice. "But I haven't the money."

"Forget it," replied Alan. "Come on, run for it."

They found an empty carriage and sat down. "We'll be in London within the hour," Alan said. "Is your uncle a church-goer, June?"

"I don't know. I don't know what he's like. I keep telling you I haven't seen him for years," replied June nervously, biting her nails.

Chapter Nine

In the train they discussed the route the ride would take. Alan had brought pen and paper and drew a map. "We will march down Castle Hill and then into the High Street; we'll turn right at the end and ride through the Market Place to the Town Hall at the top," he said. "The Mayor is opening the Arts and Crafts Exhibition at two-thirty."

"Supposing he's furious?" asked Fiona.

"Or won't come out?" inquired June.

"I shall march through the hall then and find him," replied Alan. "If there weren't steps I would ride."

"I hope nothing awful happens," June replied. "Are James and I really good enough to carry a banner?"

"We are going to practise all the week," Alan replied. "What else can we do anyway? Or do you want the riding school to go?"

June shook her head and they all sat contemplating the future till they saw tall, grey houses, washing hanging in windows and a haze of smoke and knew they had reached London.

"We can go on the Underground," said Alan, who had looked up every place he could think of on a map after breakfast. "He lives in a pretty awful part. He is an M.P., isn't he?"

June nodded. She was feeling sick. They seemed miles from the riding school now and because of that everything felt different. She did not seem to belong with the others now, hurrying after them towards the Underground, feeling strange in a dress and white socks instead of the usual jeans or jodhs.

There was hardly anyone in the Underground and they

waited a long time for a train, and as time passed June's nervousness grew. Supposing he's moved? she thought. Supposing we've come all this way for nothing. Fiona and Alan talked to one another, laughing at the advertisements pasted to the walls. James shivered and wondered whether Angela had arrived at the stables yet.

The train was half empty when it came and, when they stepped outside into fresh air again ten minutes later, it was into a long, deserted street of terrace houses.

"It's number nine," Alan said. "What a place to live!"

"Oh, they aren't bad," replied Fiona, looking at June. "We can't all live in super bungalows."

Number nine was one of the dirtiest houses in the street. Alan rang the old-fashioned door bell and then banged the door knocker, which needed polishing. "Will he recognise you?" he asked June.

June shook her head. "He may have moved," she said, shivering though the day was hot now and there was hardly a cloud in the sky.

"Oh no, that would be too awful," Alan said.

But now they could hear someone fumbling with the door.

"Who's there?" An old man shuffled down the passage and opened the door.

Alan pushed June forward. "I'm your great niece. Are you Uncle Stan?" she asked. "I've come up to see you and these are my friends, Alan, Fiona and James."

"Which one are you? I have so many nieces," he replied, peering at her. "But come inside, all of you. We can't talk in the street." He was wearing bedroom slippers and had grey hair. His green cardigan had two buttons missing. "It isn't much of a place, not since my wife died," he said, shutting the door after them.

He took them into the front room which had nothing in it besides a few chairs, table and chest of drawers.

"We thought you might be able to help us, sir," Alan said. "I believe you are an M.P."

"I was, my boy, but I'm not now," the old man said. "I lost my seat at the last election. I shan't contest another, I'm too old now, much too old . . . Oh yes, I was an M.P. for fifteen years and a shop steward before that."

"We came about our riding school," June said. "They are going to close it down and build flats. It's a super riding school and Angela who runs it is going mad with worry."

"We are getting up a petition," added Alan. "Would you sign it for us, sir?" He held out a copy. "We are going to march on the Town Hall too," he continued. "We are going to deliver it personally to the mayor."

The old man took the petition. "You've got spirit, I must say, and I like that," he replied. "Now tell me everything slowly." His hands shook and Alan felt rage rising inside him as he talked. . . . All this for nothing, he thought. And June sensed his rage and was ashamed for her great uncle. James thought, poor June, it isn't her fault, he's old and useless. She didn't know.

After a time Uncle Stan fetched them a box of sweets and said, "Share them out on the train. I've got everything straight now in my mind, but I don't know what I can do. But I'll think and something may come of it, one never knows."

Alan said, "Thank you, sir, we are very grateful to you," though he was sweating all over with suppressed anger.

"Remember me to Mother and all your little brothers and sisters, June," said Great-uncle Stan, opening the front door. "And thank you for coming. It's not often I entertain youngsters nowadays."

Alan did not speak for two minutes, not until they were out of earshot of the house. Then he cried, "All this way for nothing! He's not an M.P. You heard what he said. He can't do anything, that's obvious." He glared at June, who started to cry.

"Do shut up being so beastly," Fiona said. "It isn't

June's fault. How was she to know that he had stopped being an M.P?"

"I don't know why he gave us sweets," Alan continued, striding furiously ahead. "We are not little kids."

"You needn't eat them," Fiona replied.

"You don't understand. I bought James's ticket too. I've paid twice over," Alan said.

"You mean your mother has," retorted Fiona.

. . . . .

They had to wait a long time for an Underground train and even longer at Paddington. And no one had brought money for lunch. June cried into a small handkerchief with flowers on it. James imagined Angela arriving at the riding school, saying, "Where is everybody?" Everything will be in a mess, he thought, and she will be so disappointed. She'll see the bricks too by the notice board, he thought, and she'll know we are losing the battle.

"There's the train. Come on, run," said Alan.

They did not speak much on the journey home. Alan could only think of beastly things to say and Fiona was imagining herself selling Buccaneer. June was hating her uncle for giving them sweets, for treating Alan like a child when he was so obviously almost grown up. It did not occur to her that Alan might be being unpleasant—she blamed herself and her uncle for everything. I should have written to him first, she thought. I'm always so incompetent. But why didn't he let Mum know he had lost his seat?

"The march has got to go all right. It's our last chance," said Alan suddenly. "If anyone runs away or falls off, I shall kill him or her. I'm going to lead. You've only got to keep in line and Fiona will keep you together at the back. All you will need to do is to sit firm and use your legs."

"Yes, Alan," said James after a short silence. "We will do our best."

"Here we are," said Fiona getting up. "I wonder whether Angela is still there."

.   .   .   .   .

"Where is everyone?" asked Angela, looking round the yard. "They are usually all here on Sundays."

"Naomi and Nancy telephoned. They had to see their Granny. The others went away to catch a train. Did you see the bricks by the notice board?" asked Susan, who was one of those people who always says the wrong thing.

"Yes, hideous, aren't they?" replied Angela wiping a tear from her eye. "A sort of sacrilege. This place has been like heaven for me ever since I can remember. It broke up my marriage. I couldn't give it up and now it's being taken from me by force."

"People have got to have houses, haven't they?" replied Susan. "Times change. The rich are dying out. I wouldn't mind a flat here when I get married. Just the job."

"I should have thought one of them would have stayed," Angela said. She felt in a daze. She had wandered away from reality and she found it hard to come back, to face up to Merlin's broken knees, and the bricks waiting like locusts to invade the fields.

"Here comes James," Susan said.

He stood waving, looking alien and forlorn, thinking, I'm in time after all. "We went to London, Angela," he called, starting to run. "I was afraid I would miss you."

"I'm coming out for good soon," Angela said. "Though I'm not sure I want to really. I needn't think about anything there."

"You look better," said James, staring into her face. "Did you have a good trip to London?"

"No, awful." He did not know how much he could tell her without annoying the others. "It wasn't any

91

good," he added. "Did you see the bricks? We moved them out of the top field. I must go now, Angela. I've missed my dinner and I went out without asking anyone. I came to see if you were back."

He knew his parents would be waiting for him. He would be in terrible trouble, but it would not be the first time.

"I'll be here tomorrow," he said and turned away down the drive stopping only to shout, "Did you hear about Fiona and Buccaneer? They won."

His parents were waiting for him, standing very straight and angry on the steps of the basement.

"And where did you go?" his father called. "Slinking out like that without a word to anyone."

*   *   *   •   *

Fiona walked slowly home worrying about the march. Supposing the police stop us? Or the people with their own ponies don't want to come after all? We must have twenty people for the march; less will be ineffectual. she thought. She felt tired now and disappointed. And when she reached the manor, Paul was in the hall waiting for her.

"I thought you were never going to turn up. Why on earth did you go to London?" He was wearing a pink shirt and grey trousers.

"We went to see an M.P. about the stables," Fiona answered.

"Did you know you were in the paper this morning?" her father called. "Come and look."

She read: 'Miss Fiona Luckland won the Junior Event at Stanbridge yesterday on her bay gelding Buccaneer. She rode an excellent dressage test and jumped faultlessly across country. This is obviously a combination to be watched.' There was a photograph of her clearing the timber wagon. It made it look much higher than it really was, and she was leaning forward with her heels down, her hands halfway up Buccaneer's neck, looking determined and slim.

"It's marvellous, isn't it?" her mother asked, leaning over her smelling of perfume. "I'm going to take it to the W.I. on Wednesday. I'll take a copy of your petition too and see who will sign. How did the trip to London go?"

"Hopeless. He isn't an M.P. any more. Is there any lunch left? I'm absolutely starving," replied Fiona.

"He isn't an M.P. any more," cried June, flinging open the flat door. "Why didn't you know? Alan was furious. He treated Alan like a child. It was awful—the most awful day of my life." She looked out of the window and saw Angela standing in the stable yard talking to a pupil. "She's back!" she shouted. "I'm going . . ."

"Your dinner is waiting for you in the oven," called her mother. "We had a joint."

But June was racing down the stairs, across the road, along the drive. Angela was just going into the lodge when she reached the stable yard. "Hullo," she shouted. "Are you going to stay for good now?"

Angela shook her head. She looked pale and smelt of antiseptic. "Not till next week-end," she replied. "Isn't it boring? I still keep coming up in spots," she said.

"It was all a wash up. He's not an M.P. at all. He lives in a ghastly house and he had taken his teeth out," Alan said. "Did you keep me some lunch?"

He felt disagreeable. There were only ten days of the holidays left and in the spring he would be doing his

93

O levels. "By the way I want to go in the Army. I've decided at last," he said. "I hope you are pleased."

"That's splendid," his father replied. "By the way we took your petition with us to the New Inn and got you another ten signatures."

He felt absurdly grateful. "Of course I don't mind. Thank you very much," he replied.

"I'm going to play snooker at the Club this evening, so I will take it along with me. We care about the riding school too you know," his father said.

Chapter Ten

The next morning they practised the march in the top field. Alan brought the banners with him. Melissa, who had fair hair held back in a pony tail, volunteered to join in on her pony Horlick. Alan conscripted five other riders on their own ponies, Margaret and Jean on their two skewbalds Roulette and Poker, John on his fat Exmoor Georgie, and Peter and Andrew on grey Snowy and Highwayman. Firefly and Buccaneer were resting so June and James led on Flotsam and Jetsam, followed by Naomi on Seagull and Nancy on Jasmine; then came Margaret and Jean, John on his own and Peter and Andrew together.

"It's not really enough," complained Alan. "Do you think we can get some walkers as well? What about your mother with all her brood, June? They would look fabulous."

"Yes, they would, especially if your mother had a pram with a banner on it," suggested Fiona.

"She's not very keen," replied June, "but I'll try."

"What about your parents, James?" asked Alan.

James shook his head. "They don't like people looking at them, Alan," he replied.

"We've got a baby sister. Perhaps Mummy would come with her in the push chair," suggested Margaret.

"There's still Trooper over. Why doesn't Naomi ride him and we can get a Mum to lead her tot on Seagull," Fiona said.

"Do you think I can manage Trooper?" Naomi asked.

"Well, you've ridden him down to the bottom fields enough times," Alan replied.

"No, I haven't. I never have."

"Have Tomtit then."

Naomi ran to the stables to tack up Tomtit. He wore a double bridle and she had difficulty in getting it on. She cantered him across the top meadow and re-joined the others.

"That's twelve riders now," Alan said, holding Seagull. "If we can get twelve foot marchers as well, it won't look too bad."

"I think they should carry forks and pitchforks," Fiona said. "Or look horsy in some way or other."

"My brother and sisters don't look horsy. They look scruffy," June replied.

"I've got a toy horse on wheels. One of them can push him," Fiona suggested.

"If they come at all," replied Alan. "Come on, let's try the ride again with banners. June and James, you can carry SAVE THE RIDING SCHOOL."

It was very hot, the hottest September for years, people were saying. It seemed impossible that the summer would ever end. June took one end of the banner. I know Mum won't want to join the march, she thought.

Flotsam was very good. He seemed proud to be leading with the banner. He arched his neck and dropped his jaw, and suddenly he was between June's hands and legs going like a well-schooled dressage horse. Jetsam was going well too.

"Keep your knees level. Jolly good," shouted Alan. "We'll stop now. We'll have a full dress rehearsal on Thursday. We'll have to make some more banners before then. Do you think you can carry one between you?" He was looking at Margaret and Jean. They lived on a farm and came on Mondays and Fridays, hacking the four miles to the riding school together.

"We'll try," Margaret replied, smiling a smile which showed all her teeth. "We'll practise at home tomorrow, won't we, Jean?"

96

Jean nodded. "But we must go now," she said. "It's nearly one o'clock."

"It went quite well, didn't it?" Alan asked Fiona, and he felt more cheerful than he had for days. "I think we'll win yet," he added. "My parents are collecting signatures."

"So are mine," Fiona answered. "Things seem to be moving at last."

Susan was waiting in the stableyard. "They are taking the old lady away," she said. "They want to demolish the house."

Two large cars were parked in the drive behind the lodge. A man and a woman were helping Angela's aunt down the steps in front of her house.

Fiona and Alan ran towards them. "You can't do that," shouted Alan. "You can't take her away by force."

"It's all right dear, I want to go," replied Angela's aunt. "The place has got too big for me. They are taking me somewhere quiet where I won't have to worry."

"There's going to be an inquiry. We are not going to let them build," Alan replied.

"There you are, I'll put a rug round your knees." The old lady was in the car now. "Goodbye, children," she said, waving. "Be good."

"I'm not a child," said Fiona.

"Exactly. But what a let down," replied Alan. "Why did she want to go?"

"Heaven only knows."

"We've lost another round," said Fiona in a flat voice.

"We'll win the last one and that's what matters."

"There isn't much time." They walked back to the stables slowly like broken people. "I wish we could smash up those bricks; they don't let one forget what's coming even for a moment, do they?" asked Fiona.

"Supposing they start demolishing the big house tomorrow?"

"Boy, how I hate them."

97

"If only Angela had fought more."

The ponies were eating their lunch. "I wish it was Saturday tomorrow," Fiona said. "It's awful having to wait so long. Anything can have happened by then."

"We must put up fortifications, block the drive."

"With what?"

"An old car or something."

"My cousin's got an old car he wants to dump," said June. "It's an old Austin. The tyres are flat but we can pump them up."

"What about the pupils?" asked Fiona. "How will they get here?"

"They will have to walk up the drive. There aren't many this week anyway."

Suddenly they began to feel better.

"When can you see your cousin?" asked Fiona.

"Tonight. He lives quite near. He's married with a little girl," June replied. "It's parked in the street and the police have stuck a notice on it. No one wants it, not even the people who sell spare parts. It's all rusty, you see." Then she thought, supposing I've got everything wrong again? Supposing it's sold after all? I shall have let them down all over again. "Of course he may have got rid of it by now, but he hadn't a few days ago," she added.

They ate their lunch and cleaned the tack. In the afternoon two five-year-olds turned up and Alan and Fiona led them out for half an hour on Seagull and Jetsam, while James washed Angela's small, battered estate car, which always had oats under the seats and mud on the pedals. Susan had gone to her caravan saying, "I always have Monday off, if I haven't had the week-end. You can settle the ponies for the night. I will see you all tomorrow."

"She's the limit, isn't she?" Naomi asked.

"Absolutely foul," agreed Nancy.

"There's no one riding The Witch and Merlin on the march," June said.

"Perhaps we should ask Professor Hunstein; he's supposed to be world-famous," suggested Naomi.

"But he would want to organise it," replied Nancy. She and Naomi set off with Tomtit, Jasmine and The Witch for the bottom field; James and June started doing afternoon stables, mucking out, sweeping the yard. All the ponies were turned out now, though the grass had stopped growing and there were cracks in the earth, and dust where in the winter there was mud.

"Look, June," cried James presently, putting down the broom he was using. "Look over there. Can't you see? There are men in the top field. They are knocking in pegs." Sweat had broken out on his forehead. He had been hot all afternoon, but this was different, he could feel alarm spreading through him till his legs felt weak. "What shall we do, June?"

"I wish Alan and Fiona had come back; they always know what to do."

"They are marking out where the houses will go," James continued. "They don't even care about the ponies being in the field," June said. "And Angela not being here," added James.

They stood and stared and they both knew what they had to do.

"It's no good standing," said James after a short silence.

They walked along the drive and James's legs felt weaker and weaker and he kept thinking, if only Alan was here.

Then June called, "You can't do that here," and her courage came back and suddenly she was running, climbing the big gate into the top field, calling, "This belongs to the riding school. It's private property."

The men had rolled up the sleeves of their shirts. Their faces were red from bending. They straightened their backs.

"Run along now," one of them said. "We're busy. We have our instructions and we mean to stick to them."

The other man started measuring with a tape just as though June and James had never appeared. June could feel tears smarting at the backs of her eyes.

"There's going to be an inquiry and we've got a petition. Next week you will have to pull them all up again, you'll see; you'll wish you had listened to us then," June said.

"We'll wait till then, shall we?" replied the man, starting to knock in a peg.

"It's hopeless, June," said James as they walked back along the drive.

"You didn't say anything," replied June.

"My legs were like water."

Later when Fiona and Alan had returned and the men had gone, they returned to the field. They pulled up the pegs and broke them across their knees. They threw them at the bricks by the notice board, laughing rather hysterically.

"If Daddy saw us now he would kill us," Nancy said.

"I don't care," replied Naomi. "Let's see how far I can throw this one."

"Only four more days to the march," said Alan and they knew suddenly that all their hopes lay with it, that no other hope survived.

The next day they practised the march again and the day after. They made more banners and a boy called Roger offered to ride Merlin and a girl called Debby said she would ride The Witch.

June persuaded her mother to join the march. They made a banner out of an old pillowcase and wrote on it in red SAVE OUR HORSES.

No one came to search for the pegs. The weather stayed fine and it seemed impossible that it would ever end.

Beyond the riding school the comprehensive school

grew. Class-rooms stretched to the woods in the distance; goal posts were erected in a field.

"We will be going there next term," June said to James. "So will Nancy and Naomi."

"If it's finished in time," James replied.

Friday came as cloudless as the previous days. They spent the evening grooming the ponies, washing their tails, polishing the tack until you could see your face in the stirrups, and the saddles gleamed like polished mahogany. And in all of them suddenly, their blood seemed to be running faster.

"If Daddy saw us now he would kill us!" Nancy said

"I think we may be winning, because the bricks are still outside the field and there are no more pegs," Alan said.

"Touch wood," shouted Fiona.

They had been through the plans for the march a hundred times. Now they only had to wait.

"Supposing it rains?" asked June. "The banners will run."

"Mine won't," replied Alan. "I did mine with waterproof poster paint. Anyway does it look like rain?"

Planes left trails of vapour like paper streamers across the sky.

"Supposing Angela turns up and forbids it?" asked Naomi. "She's coming out tomorrow."

"We won't let her," replied Alan. "It's for her own good. We'll ignore her completely."

I shan't thought James. I will explain.

They could not stop talking about the march but in the end it was time to go home. They had put off all the pupils for the next day, because they did not want anything to distract them from their task. The petition was ready on Alan's desk. There were nine hundred and ninety-one signatures and they covered eighteen pages. He was to carry them in a saddle bag strapped to Firefly's saddle.

"It's going to be fine tomorrow for your march," his mother said the moment he was indoors. "Are you all ready?" He nodded. He did not want to eat or sit down. He kept walking up and down thinking of all the things which might go wrong, until his mother said, "Do stop, darling, you look just like a tiger in a cage."

He sat down then, imagining the moment when he presented the petition to the mayor. "I can't help feeling on edge," he said, "there's so much at stake."

?   .   ?   ?   ?

June's cousin had refused to dump his car in the riding school drive. He was another relation who had let her down. But her Mum was behind her to the hilt, though she kept saying, "I'm only doing this for you, June. I don't know what your Dad will say when he hears."

June's brothers and sisters were excited too. June would have promised them lollies, but she had not repaid the money she had taken from Rosie's money box yet.

James was keeping the whole march to himself. It was an intolerable strain. He knew everyone would look at him because he was the only coloured child in the ride, and he knew that was why Alan had made him ride in the front. He hoped his parents would stay at home, though he was certain they would hear about it soon enough from someone or other.

Naomi and Nancy were praying that their parents would not decide to take them to the seaside; their father kept looking at the sky. "Red night, shepherd's delight. What about going to the coast tomorrow?" he asked.

"There will be a traffic jam all the way," Naomi said.

"And we're sure to be sick in the car," added Nancy.

"We'll see how it is in the morning," their father replied. And Nancy nudged Naomi and whispered, "We'll be gone by then."

Fiona lay on her bed listening to her transistor radio. She did not want to think about the next day. I wish it was over, she thought, that everything was decided one way or another. The suspense is killing me.

Susan looked in the diary which was kept in the tack room. There were no pupils written down for the next day. Scrawled across the page were the words DAY OF THE MARCH. A map was hung on the wall with an arrowed red line which went down Castle Hill, up the High Street, through the Market Place to the Town Hall.

Something will go wrong. They're mad, thought Susan. But really I'm past caring. She was wearing an engagement ring and she kept turning it on her finger and thinking about a wedding dress.

Chapter Eleven

Saturday was fine. They met in the stable yard, coming through the early morning sunlight, all thinking the same thing—it's today.

"Mum's coming here at half-past two. She's told Dad she'll be shopping. She's hiding the banner in the pram. I hope Rosie behaves; she's a little monkey," June said. She wished the march was over already. There was so much that could go wrong.

Alan put the petition in a saddle bag, which he strapped to Firefly's saddle. A clock struck nine.

"It's odd without any pupils," Fiona said.

They caught the ponies. Susan appeared from the caravan. "You're in charge today," she said. "I'm going out with Mike. He's introducing me to his parents. I haven't met them yet." She smelt of talcum powder and her eyes were made up.

"We don't mind. Have a good time," replied Fiona.

"I don't know what Angela will say if she turns up," Susan continued. "She was dead against the march."

"She can't stop it now," replied Fiona.

Nothing could stop it now, not even the weather. Soon the children would appear on their own ponies. Later they would tack up. James stood wondering what his parents would say when it was over.

"We sneaked out of the house before our parents were up," said Naomi.

"Everything will seem so flat when it's over," Nancy said. "There will be nothing to think about."

"Plenty if we win," replied Fiona. "Only despair if

we lose." And now unexpectedly time seemed to be standing still. The ponies were groomed and ready by eleven and there was nothing to do. Then at twelve the riders on their own ponies started to arrive. Margaret and Jean came first on Roulette and Poker. "They look awful," Jean cried. "We walked all the way, but they are still sweating."

They were nervous too. "You know it's market day?" Margaret asked. "The Market Place will be full of stalls."

"It's meant to be market day. We want there to be lots of people about," Alan answered. "We want people to see the march. There's no point in marching down an empty street."

John, Peter and Andrew came all together with haynets slung across their backs. Snowy's hindquarters were the colour of weak tea. Fiona rushed for water and soap.

"I overslept," explained Peter. "Then Dad made me go to church. I don't know why, because I went last week; but he's got this thing about me being confirmed in our local church."

They were all suddenly merry.

"I wish we had some music for the march," Alan said.

"Banners are more effective," Fiona replied.

Roger and Debby arrived at half-past one on bicycles. Debby was fifteen with hair which hung down her back. She had a boy friend who drove a red sports car, and she planned to be a model when she was grown up. Roger had dark curly hair. His parents kept a self-service store; but he hoped to go to Oxford and read law.

"Where's Angela? Isn't she ever coming back?" asked Debby.

"Yes, today," Fiona replied, wishing that she looked like Debby.

"Melissa isn't coming; Horlick's lame," Roger said.

They tacked up at two o'clock. James was shaking all over by this time. June could see her mother leaving the flats with her two brothers, Trevor and Michael, and

105

Rosie, and the pram with Mark inside. They crossed the road and she hoped that they had remembered the banner. And the sun still shone from the endless blue sky. I hope Mum's put on her best frock, thought June, and washed everyone's faces, though I bet Trevor looks a mess by the time he reaches here.

Naomi and Nancy were looking forward to the march. "Supposing Daddy's in the Town Hall?" asked Naomi.

"He'll be furious," replied Nancy. "He'll stop our pocket money for a month."

But they did not mind, because nothing could destroy the perfection of the last few hours; nor the feeling of comradeship which had emerged during the past two weeks.

"Time to get up," said Alan presently. "Tighten your girths. Sit as straight and tall as you can, like soldiers." Mounting, he seemed to have been waiting for this moment all his life.

James's legs were so weak that he could hardly mount Jetsam, but when he was up some of his courage seemed to come back. June waved to her mother. Two other mothers had appeared pushing push-chairs. "We'll bring up the rear," they said. "Don't worry about us."

They were ready now, two by two in the yard. "We've still got a few minutes to spare," Alan said.

Fiona could feel her heart beating like a sledge hammer against her sides. They were all dressed in white shirts. Someone had given Rosie a bucket half full of oats to carry. She'll spill it, June thought. She always spills everything.

"Forward march," shouted Alan, looking at his watch. "Legs. Keep your ponies together. Don't ride on each other's tails, keep the right distance."

He was leading. Firefly arched his neck. The sunshine glinted on bits and stirrups and on the dees on saddles.

Rosie was arguing behind. She shouted, "I don't want to, Mum. I want to go home."

James's legs still felt like water. Supposing Mum's shopping? he thought. Supposing she sees me?

They unfurled the banners at the end of the drive.

"Now keep together. Use your legs," Alan said.

June and James carried SAVE THE RIDING SCHOOL. James's hand was shaking as he rode, but Jetsam and Flotsam stayed together and June's and his knees were level. June forgot her mother at the back. She forgot everything but the banner and her knee level with James's knee.

Fiona, at the end of the ride but in front of the pedestrians, thought, everything is going to be all right. God keep it that way.

Naomi felt high up on Trooper. She could see into the houses they passed. Nancy was saying, "Walk, steady," to Tomtit, who was shaking his head and snatching at the bit. They were going down Castle Hill now to the High Street. There was a policeman at the corner but he did not stop them. When they reached the traffic lights they knew there was a jam of cars building up behind them.

"Don't worry," shouted Alan. "Don't look back. We want people to see us." They halted knee to knee in perfect formation at the lights. Alan felt proud now. We're doing all right, he thought. A photographer from the local paper was in the High Street. There were shoppers everywhere now, people trying to cross the road, a bus stuck behind them, an angry driver hooting his horn.

"What a day to parade down the High Street," cried a woman with a loaded shopping bag in each hand. "Don't you know it's market day?"

"What riding school? I didn't know we had one," said a man in spectacles with a newspaper under his arm.

"Don't go too fast, a collected walk. Pass it back along the line," Alan told James and June.

Their hoofs clattered on the tarmac. Alan felt as though he led an army and now they had only to turn right into the Market Place. Firefly was getting restive and his mood seemed to pass all along the line of ponies. A small child cried, "Look at all those gee-gees, Mummy."

Rosie dropped the bucket of oats at the back and burst into tears. "It doesn't matter, duck," said her Mum, dragging her along by the hand.

Someone called, "What are you doing in the march, Mrs. Mills, with your kids and all? Whose side are you on?"

There were stalls all down the Market Place, selling fruit and vegetables, antiques, jumble, rugs and mats, buckets . . . The ponies looked at the stalls and shied and jogged. The formation became ragged. "Stick together," Alan cried. "Hold your banners up. We're nearly there."

James was having difficulty with Flotsam who had broken into a sweat. "I can't manage him, June," he said. "He's going to run away. I can't manage him in one hand."

"Don't drop the banner," June replied. "We're nearly there."

"He's frightened of the stalls," James said. "He won't walk." There was sweat running down his face now.

It's breaking up, thought Fiona desperately at the back.

Trooper was cantering at a standstill now. Tomtit was snorting. James let go of the banner. June shouted, "Don't, you idiot!"

Alan rode on without looking back, as tall and straight as a cavalryman. He could see the imposing front of the Town Hall now and nothing on earth was going to stop him. He could feel the mounting tension behind him; he knew James had dropped the banner, but he was so nearly there that he couldn't turn back now.

Tomtit was swinging his quarters from side to side. His tail caught on a jersey hanging on the canvas roof of a stall. He leapt forward and suddenly all the ponies panicked. James lost his stirrups. "I'm running away, help!" he shouted.

Tomtit, backing wildly, brought down the whole stall. Trooper collided with a man carrying a crate of apples. "For gawd's sake," shouted the man as the apples rolled across the road.

"I'm going back into the antiques. I can't stop him," shouted Naomi.

James had lost his reins. He had held on to the banner too long. He knew he was finished. I've ruined everything, they'll never forgive me, he thought and tears of desperation mixed with the sweat on his face, as Flotsam galloped past the Town Hall up Wood Street, scattering shoppers, one hoof still firmly fixed in the remains of a wooden crate.

꞉   •   ꞉   ꞉   ꞉

Fiona rode forward to take Firefly. All the colour had gone from her face. Alan walked up the steps of the Town Hall. None of them could see James any more and the owners of the clothes and antique stalls had gone for the police. We've lost, thought Fiona. We tried to do too much. If only we had left the banners at home, or avoided the Market Place, 'if only'—the saddest words in the English language.

The rest of the ride were getting back into line now. Naomi and Nancy had both dismounted. Their father was coming up New Street from the Anchor with his hat on the back of his head.

Alan found the mayor. The exhibition had not opened yet. He was putting on his chain of office and talking to a grey-haired woman.

"I wish to present this to your worship," Alan said, bowing slightly. "It is a petition in the interests of the riding school." He felt drained of emotion. He backed away from the mayor as though he was the Queen.

"Thank you very much," replied the mayor.

He wanted to run but he did not. The ponies were waiting outside, but there was no sign of James. A police van had arrived, and a policeman was diverting the traffic away from the Market Place.

"It was James's fault. He had one of the quietest ponies in the stables," Alan told Fiona, taking Firefly's reins.

Naomi's and Nancy's father was talking to the police.

"I will pay for everything. Don't worry, Inspector," he said. "These people are good customers of mine."

Flotsam was still galloping, but James had fallen off at the top of Wood Street. He lay on the road with a patch of blood spreading across his clean white shirt. Gradually a crowd collected.

"We'd better get an ambulance. He isn't conscious," said a tall slim man in jeans, loosening James's tie. "Poor little chap."

James stirred. "I couldn't stop," he muttered. "I did try, Alan. I did really. It was the banner, Alan. I couldn't hold it as well . . ."

He could sense the people crowding round him, though his eyes were still shut. Then strong arms lifted him onto a stretcher and bore him away; and the sun still shone, drying his blood on the road.

"Let's go home," said Margaret. "We aren't doing any good here. They shouldn't have put James in the front. He can't really ride."

"I'll come with you," Andrew replied. "There's something at five on telly which I don't want to miss."

"Same here," said John.

110

So all the children on their own ponies slipped away, while Alan marshalled what was left of the ride and said, "We'll go back up Wood Street." Naomi and Nancy remounted. The police had collected the banners and taken them away. They cleared Wood Street of traffic. "We don't want any more accidents," said the inspector.

They did not march in formation any more.

"It's the end," said Fiona, riding beside Alan. "There's no more hope. We're done for."

"What an advertisement for the riding school," muttered Alan.

"Look, that must be James's blood, how awful!" exclaimed Naomi, pointing at the dark patch of dried blood which was slowly collecting a covering of dust.

"Awful, but wasn't Daddy fabulous?" Nancy asked. "He dealt with everything. He paid for all the broken glass."

"We'll hear about it tonight," replied Naomi. "You wait."

"We tried to do too much," continued Fiona.

"We didn't. It was James's fault," Alan replied. "Supposing Flotsam's killed himself? He may have crashed into a bus."

She imagined his dark mane tangled round a bumper, his legs still and lifeless on the road. There seemed no end to misery.

"Let's trot," she said. "He may be anywhere by now."

"It will all be in the paper. The photographer from the local paper took it all, I saw him," said Alan in a stifled voice. "It will be in the Evening Mail."

"We've done Angela no good at all," Fiona continued.

"I wish the weather would change," cried Alan. "I'm sick of the summer." But he was not sick of the summer, only of what it had brought.

"The winter will be worse," replied Fiona. "With the ponies gone and no riding school any more."

They were nearly home again now and there was no

111

sign of Flotsam. "They took James away on a stretcher," said Debby, riding to the front. "Did you see? Perhaps he cracked his skull; but you don't seem to care."

"Of course we care," cried Fiona.

"It's all going to be in the paper, isn't it, isn't that enough?" asked Alan.

"No. You should care about James himself. He may be an idiot for life now," Debby said. "I wish I had never come. I thought it was going to be properly organised."

"Oh shut up," shouted Alan. "For goodness sake. Do you want to give us all nervous breakdowns."

They could see the stables now, the notice board, the bricks. Fiona's eyes were clouded with tears.

June was silent. She did not want to talk. She wanted the day to be over, finished with; she wanted to forget it, but she knew it would be engraved on her memory for ever. Supposing James dies? she thought. It will be all our fault. Why didn't someone forbid the march? Why didn't the police stop it? Why did we go by the Market Place? It's all Alan's fault. I hate him.

Angela had caught Flotsam. She stood waving to them as they rode up the drive. "Whatever *is* going on?" she shouted.

"What are we going to say?" asked Alan.

"The truth," replied Fiona. "There's nothing else."

. ˉ . . ˘

James was in hospital now. "I'm sorry," he said. "I held it as long as I could. I ruined everything, didn't I? I let you all down."

Then he saw that he was in a high white bed in a white room with windows all down one side. He was wearing a strange pair of pyjamas. It's a nightmare, he thought. But the pyjamas were real enough. A nurse came and felt his pulse. "You're going to get better," she said. "You had a nasty fall. Can you tell me your name?"

112

"Yes, I'm James Hoser. I live at Twelve Alfred Street," he said. "Does Mum know I'm here?"

"Not yet, but she will very soon now," replied the nurse, tiptoeing away.

So it's all true, thought James. I wish it had been a nightmare. I wish it wasn't true. I wish I could put the clock back, that it was still this morning. They'll cast me out now, he thought. They won't want me any more. They'll say, "Go back to where you came from." But I was born here. I came from here. I didn't mean to fall off. It was an accident. You can't blame people for accidents. There was a bandage round his head; one of his hands was scratched, he smelt of antiseptic. I wonder where Flotsam went, he thought. I wish I was dead, there's nothing left to live for. I shall never be a jockey now. I'm not going to the riding school ever again. Alan said he would kill me if I ran away, not that I mind if he does, but I don't want to face Angela. I couldn't bear it. His head was aching now. He felt stiff all over. There was a clock over the ward door. It said four o'clock. Is that all, he thought. I feel as though it all happened years ago.

"Is Flotsam all right?" called Fiona.

"Yes. He's broken a rein, but I've got plenty of odd reins which will do for the time being," replied Angela. "But who was riding him?"

They were in the yard now. "James," replied Fiona dismounting. "We went on a march."

"On a what?"

"We marched to the Town Hall and delivered a petition on your behalf; and James ran away," explained Alan, and now he felt exhausted. The work of the last few weeks was suddenly pointless, thrown away. There was nothing left now, but to go back to school and try to forget.

"But where is he," asked Angela.

113

"In hospital," replied Debby, untacking The Witch. "He was carried away on a stretcher. The whole march was a mistake. We left a trail of disaster behind us. Do you mind if I buzz off now? I've got a date at six."

"You had a nasty fall"

"Yes, go. Was he badly hurt?" asked Angela, turning to the others.

"There was blood on the road," replied Naomi. "A disgusting pool of it."

"We didn't see him fall off," Fiona said. She only

114

wanted to be home now, to have time to re-organise her thoughts.

"I'll ring up the hospital. Someone take Flotsam," said Angela. "It would happen to James. Didn't you know he wasn't good enough?"

"We were trying to help you," explained June.

Angela shrugged her shoulders and disappeared into the lodge.

Youths had broken the windows in the big house already. The curtains had been taken down. It looked empty and defeated, waiting only for demolition.

They turned the ponies out and Angela came back. "He's not too bad; they're contacting his parents. He's had three stitches in the side of his head," she said. "But he might have been killed . . ."

"I'm going now," said Alan. "I can't stand any more of anything. I'm sorry."

"Poor James," replied June. "He never has any luck. He held onto the banner too long."

"You mean he had to carry a banner?" cried Angela.

June nodded. "He held the other end of mine," she said.

Fiona and Alan walked down the drive together. Fiona pushed her bike, which had a puncture. They did not talk, because there seemed nothing left to say. Fiona kept swallowing tears, imagining Buccaneer being sold. For the first time in his life Alan looked forward to school.

They parted at the traffic lights. "I shan't be there tomorrow," Alan said.

"Nor me," replied Fiona.

Then as Alan turned left he called back over his shoulder, "I don't think I shall ever go there again." And now he was running. It's over, he thought, and in a strange way he felt relieved.

"Do you want any more help, Angela?" asked Nancy. The sun had brought out her freckles. She was dreading home. Daddy will be furious, she thought.

"No, I can manage, thank you," replied Angela. "You had better go home."

In the town people were talking about the march. A woman in the bus said, "Lot of nobs, that's all they are. A lot of nobs throwing their weight about."

"They shouldn't allow horses in the town. It isn't right," replied another woman.

"They knocked a pram over and the coloured boy was carried off on a stretcher," the conductor said. "They ought to be put in prison."

"Do you feel like a nob?" asked Nancy as they walked towards the Anchor.

Naomi shook her head. They knew it was funny to be called a nob, but they could not laugh; suddenly they felt as though they had all the burdens of the world on their shoulders. "I didn't know a pram had been knocked over," Naomi said.

"So you are back at last!" cried their father the moment they pushed the back door open. "Do you know your little escapade this afternoon cost me thirty pounds? What do you say to that?"

"I don't know," replied Naomi.

"We're sorry," replied Nancy.

"And my customers, what about them? What will they say?" he thundered. "And what about the coloured boy? If I could afford it I would send you both to boarding school."

Naomi saw a long corridor with a dormitory at the end. Nancy started to cry.

                     •

"I'll go now," June said. "I'm sorry everything went wrong. We meant everything to be lovely when you came back. James has been sweeping the yard every minute of the day, so that you would be pleased."

116

"I'm sorry too, but your march has been a disaster for us all," Angela replied.

"I'm going," June said.

The piles of bricks seemed to mock her as she passed. The notice board was one more blow.

Her mother was waiting for her. "How is James?" she cried. "I was so sorry for him, poor little mite."

"Not too bad," answered June. "Oh Mum, I'm sorry. I should never have made you come. It was all a ghastly mistake."

"I don't mind. I'm only sorry for you and your friends."

"James has got some stitches in his head," June continued. "I should have told him to drop the banner or taken hold of Flotsam. I'm hopeless," and suddenly she was crying and shivering at the same time, and muttering again and again, "It was awful, oh it was so awful. And there won't be a riding school any more now; and Angela was cross, terribly cross. You could see it on her face."

"Everything will turn out all right in the end, duck," her mother said, putting an arm round her shoulders. "One's luck has to change some day."

§   ·   ·   •   §

James's parents had come. They sat on each side of his white bed. They had brought flowers and chocolates like all the other visitors.

"You look real comfortable," his father said, in his voice that was so much deeper than anybody else's. "But I'm telling you, you don't go horse riding no more, not ever. You stay home with the rest of us."

And to James it was like a sentence of death.

Chapter Twelve

None of them helped at the stables on Sunday. James was still in hospital. June looked after Rosie, Trevor and Mark while her mother and father retired to the bedroom to sleep. Naomi and Nancy watched television all the afternoon. Alan went for a walk with his father. Fiona wrote a poem on Buccaneer:

> Goodbye, goodbye my darling horse,
> Cruel events must take their course.
> You must go and I must stay
> And the Borough Council have their way.
> But when the birds sing in the trees
> I'll remember your broad, flat knees,
> Your tidy ears, your large brown eye,
> And I'll sit and cry and cry.

On Monday morning June could see the first bulldozers entering the top field. They came like phantom monsters out of the morning mist and tore at the turf with huge claws.

"They've come, look," she called, staring out of the window. "Look, Mum." She felt beyond tears, like a spectator at the death of something which has been dying for a long time.

"Don't look, duck," her Mum said. "You start school Tuesday. There are sure to be lots of new girls. You'll forget."

"I won't forget Seagull as long as I live," replied June. "Nor Flotsam and Jetsam, nor Angela."

"You will. Time is the great healer. "You'll be all right, duck, with time," her mother said.

≋   ≋   ≋   •   ≋

Angela had taken the ponies out of the top field. There were five bulldozers at work and men were moving the bricks back into the field.

June stayed indoors all morning. "I can't go out. It's too awful," she said.

"Well, wash up the dishes then, while I pop down to the shop. It's nice to have you home for a change," her mother replied.

The sun was shining now. The dew had dried on the grass. All the hopeful joy of a fine September morning had disappeared. June washed the dishes, found her satchel and started to get ready for school. Rosie had pinched her india rubber. Michael had broken her ruler; and she was constantly drawn to the window as though by a magnet to view the work progressing in the top field. The stables will go next, she thought; then the old house. Perhaps they'll leave the lodge.

"They are getting on, aren't they?" asked her mother, returning presently with the shopping. "I've heard we're high up on the list for a house and it'll have a bit of garden. Won't that be lovely?"

June made no reply. The morning seemed unreal; it was years since she had spent a whole morning at home in the holidays. There were beef sausages for lunch and mashed potatoes, followed by two cut-up apple pies from the supermarket.

"My ruler is missing and my india rubber, and I need new plimsolls," she said.

"Oh dear, why didn't you tell me before? You had better pop round to Woolworths after dinner. I've got ten shillings somewhere," her mother replied. "You can get the lot there."

119

So in the afternoon June brushed her hair and walked down Castle Hill to the High Street and every few yards she could see where the ponies had left their hoof marks in the tarmac, which yesterday had been melting under the heat of the sun. They'll never go down Castle Hill again she thought. I expect Angela will have a sale, a great big sale of everything.

In Woolworths one assistant was saying to another, "Did you see all those horses in the town on Saturday? Terrible it was. I thought they were going to knock me over. They were all mixed up with The Market."

"No, but I heard," replied the other.

June bought a pair of plimsolls, an india rubber and a ruler. She was glad she was wearing a dress because no one knew she had been part of the march. She walked home slowly, gazing in the shop windows, not seeing what was there, seeing instead the stables falling, bulldozers digging up their concrete floors, men tying ropes round the big house . . . They destroy everything and call it progress, she thought. I would rather stay in our flat thank you. I don't want a house where the stables stood.

"They were protesting about the riding school being closed. But it's too late to protest; it was all wrapped up six months ago. Of course they could have gone to the Minister himself," said a man walking along the street with a lady in a summer dress.

"It was a disgusting display of bad manners anyway," the lady replied. "And why choose a Saturday?"

June was running now. In spite of her clothes she felt as though everyone was pointing at her, saying, "That's one of them." She ran up the stairs to the flat as though she was being chased. She stood panting in the doorway and her mother said, "There's a letter for you, June. It's just come. It's got a London postmark."

"A letter! But I never get a letter. Who's it from?"

"I can't tell unless you open it." Her mother was washing clothes. Later they would be hung across the kitchen to dry, or in the windows blotting out the sunlight.

June picked up the letter. Her hand was shaking. She looked out of the window and saw that men were knocking in pegs, that the bulldozers had dug trenches for drains, that the top field existed no more, because in a matter of hours it had become a building site.

She tore the envelope open. "I've never had a letter before, except on my birthday," she said, and read:

"Dear June,
                I was so very sorry I could not help you and your friends when you called."

"It's from Uncle Stan," she called, and could feel excitement rising inside her until she could stand no longer but paced the room as she read . . .

"But I gave your problem a lot of thought and to cut a long story short I wrote a letter to the headmaster of your new comprehensive school, who happens to be someone I did a good turn some years back. I suggested that the riding school could be incorporated with the new school, so making his school among the first state schools to include riding in the curriculum. I enclose his reply. As you will see he has written to your Mrs. Manners already and she is doubtless considering his proposal by now.

Do contact me again if you have any further problems.

                          Yours affectionately,
                              Great-uncle Stan."

"He's done it, he's done it," shouted June. "He's saved the riding school. Here, read the letter. I haven't read the other one but it doesn't matter. We'll be able to ride at school. We won't even have to pay. Oh I'm so happy. And they said he wasn't any good, that I had wasted their money; but he's marvellous!" She tore round and round the flat like a lunatic; then she cried, "I'm going to the riding school. I'm going to tell the others."

"What if Mrs. Manners turns it down?" suggested her mother, folding the letter.

"She can't. She won't. Oh, I had better change. I can't go in this silly frock," cried June. "We'll have to tell

"He's done it, he's done it," shouted June

James too. I can't leave him out."

Two minutes later she was running out of the block of flats, down the drive and now the bulldozers digging did not matter any more. We hated the comprehensive school too, she thought, but I don't any more. And I'm so proud of Uncle Stan.

Angela's post had come too. She was sitting in the saddle room reading her letter over and over again.

"Everything's going to be all right," she said. "The stables are all going to be moved to the comprehensive school, and later on the council may build me an indoor school, and you will all ride for nothing."

"I know. My uncle arranged it, my great-uncle Stan," June exclaimed and it seemed like a wonderful dream. "We visited him in London," she continued, "he used to be an M.P."

"I'm so pleased," Angela said. "I just can't believe it's true."

"I'm going to tell the others," cried June.

     🕮   🕮   🕮   •   •

When June knocked on the front door Alan was reading angry letters about the march in the afternoon paper. He thought oh no, *not* a visitor, and opened the door.

"Everything's going to be all right," June cried. "Come to the stables. We're going to have a celebration."

"Have you gone mad?" asked Alan, peering at her.

"Uncle Stan's saved us. I'm going to tell Fiona," cried June, turning round, disappearing down the path, while Alan felt the first stirrings of hope come back.

Fiona was having a bath. She came to the door in a dressing gown. June looked small and untidy. "Whatever is it now?" she asked. "Is Buccaneer lame or something?"

"My Uncle Stan has saved the riding school," cried June.

"What, Great-uncle Stan?" asked Fiona to gain time.

"Yes, we must have a celebration. Please telephone Naomi and Nancy."

June was going now, feeling as though she was floating on a cloud; her legs seemed to have wings as she ran back to the riding school. Rosie will be able to ride too, she thought. All my friends will be able to, and James.

Fiona started to dress. Her hands shook so that she found it difficult to do up the buttons of her shirt. She kept thinking, the nightmare's over. I can keep Buccaneer. I can be selected to ride for England if I'm good enough. Maddening tears of happiness flooded her eyes as she shouted to her mother, "Everything is all right. I can keep Buccaneer," and opened the garden gate and ran madly down the road, her hair still wet from the bath. But what can Uncle Stan have done? she thought, when she reached the drive, staring at the top field. No one can put the turf back now, and they are still building. Supposing June *has* gone mad? But she could see Alan now running ahead of her. I forgot to ring up Naomi and Nancy. I'll telephone from the lodge, she thought. What an idiot I am.

Twenty minutes later they were all there save James.

"I can take the stables with me; they're portable," Angela said, looking years younger than she had last week.

"Will you be able to teach people like me and Alan? Or only state pupils?" Fiona asked. It was something which had been worrying her for the last ten minutes.

"I'll take who I like at week-ends and in the holidays," Angela replied. "Your money will go into school funds. I am going to be paid a salary and it's more than I've ever earned in a year. And the school will provide jumps and buy more horses later as we need them."

"It's the most wonderful thing which ever happened," June said. She wanted to say, "And my Great-uncle Stan arranged it all," but suddenly it was not important any more, what mattered was that the stables were going on.

But Fiona seemed to have read her thoughts, for she said, "We must write a joint thank-you to June's great-uncle. We were beastly about him and he's turned up trumps."

June didn't know what trumps mean. "It didn't matter about him not being an M.P. after all," she answered.

Alan was drawing a plan in the diary of a yard and stables and a covered school.

"No one has told James yet, and he cared as much as any of us and he must be feeling awful. He must be thinking he's let us all down. I'm so sorry for him," Naomi said.

She and Nancy would be going to the new comprehensive school as well as James and June. She still felt dazed by the news. She tried to imagine Angela writing reports like the other teachers. I expect we'll be able to choose between hockey and riding, she thought.

"Can't we visit him?" June asked.

"He may not be home yet. I'll go and telephone the hospital," Angela replied.

While she was inside the lodge they stood gazing at the comprehensive school, which was still growing, eating up the landscape, changing it for ever. And now they did not hate it; suddenly it seemed full of promise.

˘   ˇ   §   •   ß

"You will be going home tomorrow," a nurse said. "So you can get up and sit in a chair while I make your bed, and you can sit at the table for supper this evening."

"I don't want to go home," James replied. "I like it here." He wondered what he would do all day when he was home again. He did not want to be with the other boys playing football in the street. He had no friends, because until now he had spent every spare moment in his life at the riding school. When he had wanted to discuss anything, he had discussed it with Angela in the tack room. He had not needed friends until now.

"I want to stay here for ages," he told the nurse, who ruffled his hair, muttering, "Silly boy," and started to make another patient's bed while he sat looking at a man in bed with both his arms in plaster. A West Indian nurse said, "So you don't want to go back home, eh? You're a silly boy then. You should like your home." And James could not find words to explain what had happened, how he had failed everyone, and would never be able to look Alan or Fiona in the face again. I shall hide if I see them coming down the street, he thought. I shall wear different clothes so that they won't recognise me.

"And now you are to put on a dressing gown and go outside the ward," the nurse continued. "It is special orders. You have friends coming to see you. It is all most irregular, but it seems a lady knows the doctor; so they are making a special case of you. But you must be in the passage. We can't have all our patients disturbed."

It must be something to do with the march, thought James. Somebody's coming to say it was all my fault.

.   .   .   .   .

"I've been talking to Doctor Baker. He's making a special concession. I told him James was probably making himself sick with worry and guilt." Angela was laughing for the first time in weeks. "Come on, we'll take the car and stop and buy chocolates."

The car would not start until they had pushed it half-way down the drive. Then they all piled in and June said, "I've never been in a hospital before, not even to see Mum when she had Mark."

"Nor have I," replied Fiona.

"I had my tonsils out when I was six, but I went into a nursing home," Alan said.

They were nearly at the hospital now.

"I hope he doesn't look too awful," Naomi said. "I'm not very good about blood. Lots of it makes me sick."

Angela turned the car off the road onto a sweep of gravel.

"Here we are," she said. "Now walk, don't run, and talk quietly; remember where you are."

"Aye aye," replied Naomi.

126

They walked down a long corridor smelling of anti-septic and found James at the end of it, sitting half lost in a large armchair, in a hospital dressing gown, pyjamas and slippers. He looked small, forlorn, like a frightened animal.

He opened his mouth to say, "I'm sorry," but at the same moment they all started talking, leaping up and down saying, "It's all right, the riding school's saved. It's being moved to the comprehensive school. You'll be able to ride at school. June's uncle saved it . . ."

He looked at Angela and she nodded and he felt happiness coming back, loosening the tenseness in his body. "So everything is going to be all right?" he asked. "It didn't matter me falling off? But what about Flotsam, Angela?"

"He was all right," Angela replied. "Everything's all right, including me, so hurry up and get well, because I can't manage without you."

"The stables are going to be moved too," June cried. "Everything, and there may be an indoor school." She was jumping up and down again and a sister came down the passage and tapped her on the shoulder, "Not so much noise," she said.

"We had better be going now," Angela said. "Here are a few chocolates, James. "Get well soon."

"I shall be home tomorrow, Angela," James answered. "I only have sticking plaster, no bandage now," and suddenly he was laughing, seeing himself cantering across green fields, riding in a covered school with all the lights shining out across dark fields. I'll ride in horse trials, he thought, looking at the chocolates, not seeing the others going away down the long white corridor, turning to wave at the end. They are all my friends, he thought, my friends for ever, and now he wanted to go home, for suddenly every second spent in the hospital was a wasted second.

Later the others danced round a bonfire and sang.

Angela, Fiona and Alan drank cider, raising their glasses and crying, "To the new riding school." And June, looking towards her own home, thought, we've got the best of both worlds, a better house for Mum and Dad and for James and his family, and the stables as well and, when Mark and Rosie and Trevor and Michael are older, they will be able to ride as well and all for nothing.

Fiona was thinking, I will be able to keep Buccaneer here for ever. I shall be able to school him in the covered school in winter, and Angela will go on teaching me and there seemed no end to her happiness.

Alan thought, if all the local children ride they will become nicer and maybe I shall be able to take my A levels at the new school and live at home and Dad can spend the money he saves on education on a cross-country horse as good as Buccaneer.

Naomi and Nancy were unable to put their happiness into words. It was something which seemed to grow inside them until they wanted to rush round the town shouting to everyone, "It's saved. It's going on. It's here for ever."

"The authorities aren't so bad after all," Angela said, gazing across the fields to where the new school stood, seeing herself with endless pupils, new saddles, more horses, a new life.